Hostage to Death

SELECTED FICTION WORKS BY L. RON HUBBARD

FANTASY
The Case of the Friendly Corpse
Death's Deputy
Fear
The Ghoul
The Indigestible Triton
Slaves of Sleep & The Masters of Sleep
Typewriter in the Sky
The Ultimate Adventure

SCIENCE FICTION
Battlefield Earth
The Conquest of Space
The End Is Not Yet
Final Blackout
The Kilkenny Cats
The Kingslayer
The Mission Earth Dekalogy*
Ole Doc Methuselah
To the Stars

ADVENTURE
The Hell Job series

WESTERN
Buckskin Brigades
Empty Saddles
Guns of Mark Jardine
Hot Lead Payoff

A full list of L. Ron Hubbard's
novellas and short stories is provided at the back.

*Dekalogy—a group of ten volumes

L. RON HUBBARD

Hostage to Death

Published by
Galaxy Press, LLC
7051 Hollywood Boulevard, Suite 200
Hollywood, CA 90028

Printed in the United States of America.

ISBN-10 1-59212-282-5
ISBN-13 978-1-59212-282-0

Library of Congress Control Number: 2007927539

Contents

Stories from Pulp Fiction's Golden Age

A ND it *was* a golden age.
The 1930s and 1940s were a vibrant, seminal time for a gigantic audience of eager readers, probably the largest per capita audience of readers in American history. The magazine racks were chock-full of publications with ragged trims, garish cover art, cheap brown pulp paper, low cover prices—and the most excitement you could hold in your hands.

"Pulp" magazines, named for their rough-cut, pulpwood paper, were a vehicle for more amazing tales than Scheherazade could have told in a million and one nights. Set apart from higher-class "slick" magazines, printed on fancy glossy paper with quality artwork and superior production values, the pulps were for the "rest of us," adventure story after adventure story for people who liked to *read*. Pulp fiction authors were no-holds-barred entertainers—real storytellers. They were more interested in a thrilling plot twist, a horrific villain or a white-knuckle adventure than they were in lavish prose or convoluted metaphors.

The sheer volume of tales released during this wondrous golden age remains unmatched in any other period of literary history—hundreds of thousands of published stories in over nine hundred different magazines. Some titles lasted only an issue or two; many magazines succumbed to paper shortages during World War II, while others endured for decades yet. Pulp fiction remains as a treasure trove of stories you can read, stories you can love, stories you can remember. The stories were driven by plot and character, with grand heroes, terrible villains, beautiful damsels (often in distress), diabolical plots, amazing places, breathless romances. The readers wanted to be taken beyond the mundane, to live adventures far removed from their ordinary lives—and the pulps rarely failed to deliver.

In that regard, pulp fiction stands in the tradition of all memorable literature. For as history has shown, good stories are much more than fancy prose. William Shakespeare, Charles Dickens, Jules Verne, Alexandre Dumas—many of the greatest literary figures wrote their fiction for the readers, not simply literary colleagues and academic admirers. And writers for pulp magazines were no exception. These publications reached an audience that dwarfed the circulations of today's short story magazines. Issues of the pulps were scooped up and read by over thirty million avid readers each month.

Because pulp fiction writers were often paid no more than a cent a word, they had to become prolific or starve. They also had to write aggressively. As Richard Kyle, publisher and editor of *Argosy,* the first and most long-lived of the pulps, so pointedly explained: "The pulp magazine writers, the best of them, worked for markets that did not write for critics or attempt to satisfy timid advertisers. Not having to answer to anyone other than their readers, they wrote about human beings on the edges of the unknown, in those new lands the future would explore. They wrote for what we would become, not for what we had already been."

Some of the more lasting names that graced the pulps include H. P. Lovecraft, Edgar Rice Burroughs, Robert E. Howard, Max Brand, Louis L'Amour, Elmore Leonard, Dashiell Hammett, Raymond Chandler, Erle Stanley Gardner, John D. MacDonald, Ray Bradbury, Isaac Asimov, Robert Heinlein—and, of course, L. Ron Hubbard.

In a word, he was among the most prolific and popular writers of the era. He was also the most enduring—hence this series—and certainly among the most legendary. It all began only months after he first tried his hand at fiction, with L. Ron Hubbard tales appearing in *Thrilling Adventures, Argosy, Five-Novels Monthly, Detective Fiction Weekly, Top-Notch, Texas Ranger, War Birds, Western Stories,* even *Romantic Range.* He could write on any subject, in any genre, from jungle explorers to deep-sea divers, from G-men and gangsters, cowboys and flying aces to mountain climbers, hard-boiled detectives and spies. But he really began to shine when he turned his talent to science fiction and fantasy of which he authored nearly fifty novels or novelettes to forever change the shape of those genres.

Following in the tradition of such famed authors as Herman Melville, Mark Twain, Jack London and Ernest Hemingway, Ron Hubbard actually lived adventures that his own characters would have admired—as an ethnologist among primitive tribes, as prospector and engineer in hostile climes, as a captain of vessels on four oceans. He even wrote a series of articles for *Argosy*, called "Hell Job," in which he lived and told of the most dangerous professions a man could put his hand to.

Finally, and just for good measure, he was also an accomplished photographer, artist, filmmaker, musician and educator. But he was first and foremost a *writer*, and that's the L. Ron Hubbard we come to know through the pages of this volume.

This library of Stories from the Golden Age presents the best of L. Ron Hubbard's fiction from the heyday of storytelling, the Golden Age of the pulp magazines. In these eighty volumes, readers are treated to a full banquet of 153 stories, a kaleidoscope of tales representing every imaginable genre: science fiction, fantasy, western, mystery, thriller, horror, even romance—action of all kinds and in all places.

Because the pulps themselves were printed on such inexpensive paper with high acid content, issues were not meant to endure. As the years go by, the original issues of every pulp from *Argosy* through *Zeppelin Stories* continue crumbling into brittle, brown dust. This library preserves the L. Ron Hubbard tales from that era, presented with a distinctive look that brings back the nostalgic flavor of those times.

L. Ron Hubbard's Stories from the Golden Age has something for every taste, every reader. These tales will return you to a time when fiction was good clean entertainment and the most fun a kid could have on a rainy afternoon or the best thing an adult could enjoy after a long day at work.

Pick up a volume, and remember what reading is supposed to be all about. Remember curling up with a *great story.*

—Kevin J. Anderson

KEVIN J. ANDERSON *is the author of more than ninety critically acclaimed works of speculative fiction, including* The Saga of Seven Suns, *the continuation of the Dune Chronicles with Brian Herbert, and his* New York Times *bestselling novelization of L. Ron Hubbard's* Ai! Pedrito!

Hostage to Death

CHAPTER ONE

The Challenge of the Hand

THE severed hand lay upon the scarred desk, its fingers lifted and curled, as though raising its palm in mute supplication. Drained of blood, the severed tendons and arteries stood out at the wrist—hollow white tubes. The man who had cut off that hand had done it neatly, as though he had been carving a fowl, instead of human flesh. The wrist joint protruded, white and glistening.

For dragging seconds no one in the hut moved. And then Lieutenant Reilly found breath enough to gasp, "Good God!" He stared around him at the tense faces of the Legionnaires. Their eyes were drawn to the thing like steel to a magnet.

"Call divisional PC," said Lieutenant Reilly.

Sergeant Morenz, his weathered face stiff, said, "The wires are down, sir, I was just coming in to tell you when the runner brought—brought that."

Lieutenant Reilly looked back at the grisly object. It had been wrapped in cheap paper, and upon the paper, like worms crawling over cloth, was a set of Arabic words.

Picking up a rifle cleaning rag, Reilly removed the object and looked at the writing. Arabic was no great mystery to him, but this was blurred. The message read:

Sergeant Morenz, his weathered face stiff, said,
"The wires are down, sir, I was just coming in to tell you when
the runner brought—brought that."

To Railguard Three:

I beg to inform you that I am holding a certain Englishwoman named Kay MacArthur. I send this to you today. Tomorrow I shall send you one of her hands. I do this because I seriously doubt your courage and the fighting quality of your men, who do nothing but cringe beside a railroad, watching the trains. Come and get Kay MacArthur.

Blessings from Abd el-Ulad

Lieutenant Reilly went to the door and looked southwest, to the uneven blue-white humps which were the High Atlas. In the midsummer heat, the brown plains shimmered and writhed on their way to the foothills.

Stepping outside, Reilly stared to the north. The iron and cinders that made up the roadbed were scorching hot under the metallic, brittle sky. The great cauldron of molten copper that was the sun beat the parched earth with searing rays.

Sergeant Morenz had finished reading the message when Reilly came back. Sergeant Morenz, his tunic soggy and dark with sweat, shrugged.

"It is to be pitied, *mon Lieutenant.* Unable as we are to reach battalion, we can do nothing. Yes, it is to be pitied."

Reilly's black eyes went suddenly hot. "Are you trying to tell me what to do? Get the hell out of here and down to your barracks!"

They went, those Legionnaires. Hurriedly. One of them grinned a bit when he was outside and whispered to another, "*Sacrebleu,* little pig, it will not be long."

"No, not long. When he swears, *zut*! We have action! I am weary of this railhead, me."

Sergeant Morenz lingered near the door, hesitantly. He felt very responsible, did Morenz. It showed in his sunken, colorless eyes.

Lieutenant Reilly fidgeted and stared down at his dusty boots, frowning. He pulled out his revolver and whirled its cylinder, then replaced it. He went to his desk, glared at the offending hand and reread Abd el-Ulad's message.

"Morenz!" cried Reilly. "Get in here!"

Morenz re-entered and saluted.

Reilly did a turn around the walls of the iron-roofed furnace which passed for his quarters and came back to Morenz. "Sergeant, what were our orders when we came to this place?"

"Sir," said Morenz, "our orders were these: Guard the railhead at post three. Under no pretext are you to leave this post. The railhead is all important."

"Go on," said Reilly.

Morenz relaxed a little. "I'm thinking, begging the lieutenant's pardon, about Captain Francois deGrille. You remember the captain, don't you, Lieutenant? He left Fort Germaine, down in the Sahara. Went after a woman, he did, sir. Captain deGrille, begging the lieutenant's pardon again, will be sentenced next week, sir. I need not remind you, *mon Lieutenant,* that *la belle Légion* is a very jealous lady."

"Rats!" said Lieutenant Reilly. "DeGrille was a fool. He had his entire post wiped out by Tuaregs in his absence. We aren't at war with anyone. The Riffs are after the Spaniards, not the French."

"As the general said on parade last month, *mon Lieutenant*, 'All Morocco is blazing with revolt.'"

"That's trite," cried Reilly. "Damned trite! It's been blazing with revolt ever since they landed us here. And how many engagements have we fought? None!

"Morenz, this Abd el-Ulad—he's a Berber. Just a guerrilla warrior. That other fellow—what's his name? Abd el-Krim—won't have anything to do with him. This Ulad wants to wipe out a Legion company and thereby gain favor in the eyes of Krim. He thinks he's got a setup, this Ulad.

"Well, Morenz, this Ulad is going to be fooled. We're going up and *wipe him out*!"

"*Mon Lieutenant!*" cried Morenz. "It means deserting your post!"

"You, a sergeant, are telling me what to do?"

Morenz backed hastily away. This Reilly was a fighter, not to be tampered with. Down in the Sahara, this Reilly had a reputation. When those black eyes grew wild, such lesser things as sergeants did well to get out of the way. Morenz got. He knew the conflict. It wasn't human to leave a woman in Berber hands without doing something about it.

But then, since when was warfare human?

Lieutenant Edouard William deReilly, as he was listed on the Legion books, went to the window and looked out across the scaly, sun-scourged plain. Up there Abd el-Krim was going at it hammer and tongs with the Spaniards.

Not long before, Reilly remembered, the Spanish general, Silvestre, had lost his six thousand Spanish soldiers in the siege of the Mountain of Baran. Shot down like sheep by Riffian guns, the six thousand corpses had strewn the slopes of Baran and the vale by the tomb of *Sīdī* Misaud el-Derkawi.

Silvestre had blown out his brains with his own pistol, rather than suffer either capture or explanation to the king.

Reilly remembered with a twinge that Silvestre had been acting independently, *without orders or support.*

Yes, the Riffs were at it again up there. Fighting to drive the Christians into the sea. Reilly thanked God that France wasn't in it—not yet. The closest France had come had been in connection with this railroad over which passed nightly trains of Spanish supplies and troops from other sectors. Guarded, paradoxically, by the French Foreign Legion, because France didn't want the Riffs to tear up the rails.

Reilly looked back at the severed hand and shoved shaky fingers into his tunic pocket to bring forth a sweat-dampened pack of vile Algerian cigarettes. It was a bad situation, a hard decision, because a man of Reilly's ancestry is shot through and through with a streak of romanticism as wide as a mountain river and as hard to control.

Lieutenant Edouard William deReilly was not French at all. He was, for the time being, a citizen of France. He had graduated from that mighty school St. Cyr, where army officers are made for the tricolor. He had fought his campaigns and won his medals and ribbons with both Spahis and Legion, in both mountain and desert jungle.

His grandfather had been a captain of the Irish Guard—the French stand and cheer when you mention that part of their military history. They tell you that the gentlemen of Ireland fought superbly and gallantly for France through scores of years. The first deReilly had been, of course, O'Reilly, but the name had shifted. The women of the family had all come from Ireland, except Reilly's mother. She was an American.

Three years before his father had died at the first battle of Verdun, Reilly's mother had taken him back to America where, for the better part of his youth, he had been plain Bill Reilly, "that exceptionally hard-boiled, gentlemanly little boy."

He had come back to France to attend St. Cyr, and for the past two years he had been mopping up Africa—France's granary—to France's profit and his own delight.

As an officer of *la belle Légion,* he was respected, hailed and fêted. For, though France thinks little of the enlisted Legionnaire, she knows that the officers are the finest, the best and positively the most romantic gentlemen extant—perhaps with the exception of the *Chasseurs Alpins.*

Thus, it was hard for Bill Reilly to turn his back on that hand. An Irish gentleman to the core, with an American's straightforward impulsiveness, Reilly was finding it impossible to turn down the challenge.

Should anything happen to that railhead in his absence—well, they wouldn't be able to find dungeons deep enough or bars too thick. On the surface, France and Spain were friends.

His black eyes and black hair, his compact, pug-nosed face, his deceptive slenderness, stood Reilly in good stead here in a dark country. He could forage for news with a djellaba about his shoulders, passing himself off for an Arab or even a Berber.

For wild minutes he stood there, thinking that he would stand a better chance if he went up to this hideout by himself, disguised as a Riff. He knew he had the nerve to try it, but you had to have men to blast a fighter like Abd el-Ulad. Even sixty men would be a handful when the Sniders and Mannlichers and flintlocks began to bark. You'd need a squadron of cavalry, about seven machine guns, a plane or two—

Well, fifty Legionnaires could do it.

Reilly went out the door and glanced about him. The bugler was asleep on a bench in the questionable shade of the wall, his German face covered with globules of sweat, flies hovering perilously close to his open mouth.

"Schwartz!" cried Reilly thunderously. "You lazy—!"

Down at the barracks, the Legionnaires heard the words and grinned cheerfully. After all, it was a bore making a railroad safe for Spaniards. And this Abd el-Ulad probably needed a lesson. They knew what Reilly meant when he swore.

A good officer swears. A bad one means it.

"Schwartz!" roared Reilly again. "Let's have a few sour notes out of that tin-fish horn! We're leaving for the Atlas!"

CHAPTER TWO

Ambushed!

THE road was nothing more than a strip of thicker dust between parched fields where the grain came to a head in spite of the drought. Fifty pairs of heavy boots going up, down, up, down had stirred the flour-fine particles into an all-engulfing tan fog which hung like a miscolored shroud behind the column.

The Legion boots, square and rugged, built for men who had to move with a cavalry quickness on foot, left heavy prints, which were immediately blotted out by a wind coming down like a blast from hell's air vents.

Incongruously, the Legionnaires had only to look up at the sprawling peaks to see the clinging snow, white against a metal sky.

Marching at route step, rifles slung, equipment banging, the men watched the boots before them with dust-stung, sun-seared eyes. And the boots went up and down like the ticking of a clock—a drugging monotony of motion which made a man forget that he didn't dare touch his canteen before he knew from whence his next water was coming. In this period of drought, water holes fail and rivers forget that they try to reach the sea.

Bill Reilly walked with his men, disdaining to ride. The

lieutenant's horse could carry one more machine gun which, Reilly avowed, might be much more important than a subaltern's whistle.

Up there somewhere in the foothills, which had already begun to rise under their feet, Reilly knew Abd el-Ulad would be waiting, watching this column of dust against the afternoon sky, licking a set of very thin lips which were almost obscured by a thick brown beard. And the Berber soldiery would also be waiting, hands steady on rifles as hot as branding irons, bodies sagged easily against porous rock that would quickly blister the palm of a white man.

The boots went up and down and added dust to the shroud of dust, and the foothills began to split apart and grow alarmingly high. They were in the Atlas.

Reilly fell to wondering about Kay MacArthur. An Englishwoman, the message had said. Probably the girl who had been with that party of archeologists who had passed through Fez some four months back.

Kay MacArthur, decided Reilly, would be tall and straight, and dressed in very severe tweeds. She'd look down her nose at you and sniff quite audibly. She'd be dependable and stiff, and would undoubtedly bear out the old English tradition of never looking shocked, terrified or otherwise ruffled. She'd probably made Abd el-Ulad very angry by slapping his face.

Also, thought Reilly, she'd have a title to her name. Lady Kay MacArthur, no doubt, something-or-other of something-or-other *on* something-or-other.

Well, you still didn't let the Berbers cut off people's hands and ship them around. The poor devil who had owned that ghastly hand. . . . Reilly fell to wondering who that man might have been.

As they entered a narrow defile, something flashed in the oblique rays of the settling sun—something blue and white. Reilly raised his arm and loosed a shrill blast from his whistle.

"Deploy skirmishers!"

The Legionnaires scattered.

Dust jumped in a tan fountain, and a slug sang shrilly away from a boulder. A puff of lazy smoke was drifting away from a niche high in the pass.

The flared nose of a Legion auto-rifle jutted from the top of a rock, spitting jagged streaks of white fire through the sunlight. *Tac-tac-tac-tac!* Blurred and vicious, like the repeated cracking of a bull whip.

The niche was emptied. A brown djellaba blossomed like a fouled parachute. *"La ilahu illa Illahi! La—"* The Berber cry was cut off and dust rose in a cloud above the body. The brown robe settled slowly.

The Legionnaires were out of sight. The column of dust which still fanned through the coming dusk was all that lived or moved in the pass. The silence was leaden and unreal.

Reilly looked up at the wall. He could have sent one of his men, but a good commanding officer never orders that which he will not do himself. His crossbelts shifted on the back of his tunic as he started the climb. The holster slapped his thigh, and a worn collar insignia caught a ray of light and hurled it back like the flashing muzzle of a gun.

The hysterical whine of a slug yowled through the defile. The echoes of the report rumbled sullenly, suddenly split apart by the Legion auto-rifle. *Tac-tac-tac-tac!*

Reilly went on climbing, a good target at a hundred yards, but a bad one at five hundred. A Berber sniped with the regularity of a blacksmith's hammer. Evidently the man's rifle was a new repeater, because there came a double pause in every five shots.

Jagged splinters of stone snapped into Reilly's face. His hands were calloused, but not to the point of being invulnerable to the cutting of the rough wall.

Spangggg! The Berber was jacking up his sights, making certain of his range. The edge of the cliff was a good ten feet above Reilly's head. His arms were tired, and the holster wore his side raw.

The auto-rifle clattered spitefully. A Lebel cracked like a breaking stick. The Berber who fell did not cry out to Allah. His jaw was gone.

Running along the top of the cliff, Reilly made an excellent silhouette against the sky, even though he moved swiftly. Lead spattered up at him, moaning and whining as it ricocheted. He dropped behind a rock. His black eyes came up for a moment, surveyed the cliffs below and then disappeared. His head bobbed up in a different spot. He spat a mouthful of rock splinters and shifted again.

He reached a spot where he could see his men without making a target of himself.

"*En avant!*" he bawled. "Three men to the north wall! Ten around the end of the gorge!"

14

His words were drowned in a howl from Legion throats. The desert snipers were suddenly too busy to look up. Reilly steadied his gun hand on a boulder and fired with great care. The range was only eighty yards.

"One," he said. "Two! Three!" Smoke curled out of the long revolver muzzle. A Snider dropped fifty feet to the ravine floor. A Berber rolled off his perch, dazed by the numbing impact of a heavy slug. The third made no movement whatever.

Reilly scrambled down the face of the cliff and dropped into the wake of his charging men. They ran like sprinters, those Legionnaires, just as though they had not hiked all day without water, without rest.

The Legion auto-rifle was up above them, racketing in three-five bursts expertly placed. The Legion khaki and blue and steel went on through the defile.

A man stumbled and Reilly darted to one side to turn him over. With a shake of his head, Reilly ran on. The man needed no help—not now.

Moorish horsemen stampeded before the onslaught of Legion tri-bladed bayonets. Berbers leaned out of their saddles, firing back. The Legion auto-rifle had changed its position again—or perhaps it was another.

The desert riders piled up as though they had run into an invisible wall. Men and horses were tangled in the red-ringed dust, colored by the waning sun. The Legion auto-rifle went on without pause.

"That's enough!" cried Reilly, and the gun stopped its cackling.

Looking about him, the lieutenant saw that they had entered a clearing ringed by many houses built from logs and mud and stone. No heads at the windows, no horses in the corrals. Only a small wisp of smoke which rolled out of a dying fire.

A voice was calling, "Over here!" Reilly stopped. "Over here!" cried the voice again, cool and clear.

Reilly walked through the debris with quick, sure strides. He found time on the way to button a tunic pocket and rearrange his crossbelts.

At the doorway of the dim room, he stopped. After all, it might be some kind of trick. They might blast him down if—

He could see a small patch of white in the darkness. His heels rapped the board floor. He stopped as though on parade and made a short bow.

Now that his eyes were accustomed to the dusk, he could see her clearly. Her face was perfectly set. Her lips were full and lovely. Her eyes were large and dark and pleasing.

Reilly promptly forgot about himself. He slashed the ropes from her wrists. After that, he helped her stand up. For a full minute they stood there looking at each other.

Reilly fumbled with his handkerchief and mopped his face. "We'd . . . we'd better be getting outside, Miss MacArthur. They might come back, you know."

He led her to the door, and they walked out into the soft twilight.

The Legionnaires, posted by the orders of the sergeant, stared until they saw the expression on the lieutenant's face.

Suddenly they were very busy looking for tinned food in their packs or guarding the entrance to the pass.

"The devil with that!" cried Reilly. "Fall in! We're leaving here before Abd el-Ulad decides to come back."

Morenz stepped up with a salute. "*Pardon, mon Lieutenant.* This is very queer. It is all too easy. Shall I send out a vanguard to scout—"

"Send ten men immediately. If this Ulad swings his face up, blast him. *En avant!*"

He turned to Kay MacArthur and looked at her again. She was dressed in a white shirt and a white linen skirt. Her small feet were booted in leather that had seen better days. Her dark hair was loose and streaming down over her slim shoulders.

"There's my horse," said Reilly. "Get on and ride."

"But I'd rather—"

Yells rattled through the defile, punctuated by the stuttering snarl of machine guns.

The Legionnaire who burst into the clearing staggered, holding his side. "They've come back!" he cried. "The slope is swarming with them!"

Rifle bolts snicked. Two others of the vanguard made their way to the huts, dragging a third. They knew they were trapped, these men. All eyes turned to Lieutenant Bill Reilly.

Reilly's voice was very cold. "Fix bayonets! Machine guns forward! Morenz, cover that upper wall!"

The fighting machine swung into its grooves and started ahead. They knew that they were trapped, but they had faith

17

in Reilly. Who would have suspected that they had been allowed to filter through the main column of Abd el-Ulad?

Kay MacArthur tried to hold Reilly's sleeve. He turned, picked her up and tossed her to the back of the horse.

"Don't hang back for us," he ordered. "If you see a hole, go through it and ride like hell!"

His face looked very set in the dark. She was aware that something else was worrying him. And he was thinking about that four AM train which would be hurtling along an unguarded roadbed, crammed with soldiers. Spaniards, perhaps—but they were soldiers.

The machine guns were starting up out there again. The blaze of exploding powder lit up the walls of the defile with a flickering red light. All was lost in a tangled roar of sound.

CHAPTER THREE

Adventure Ends in Disaster

A Legionnaire of the vanguard had set up a light machine gun squarely in the mouth of the pass. He sprawled across it now, his blood running down the belt, spoiling the polish of brass cartridge cases.

Reilly thrust the man aside. It was still light enough to see the slope beyond the defile—to see a swirl of men darting from boulder to boulder, coming up like so many gray ghosts. In the night, rifles flashed in long, spark-studded red gashes.

The light machine gun began to chatter. Reilly held its jolting butt and sprayed fire through a forty-five-degree arc. Somewhere near, Morenz was swearing in a cracked voice. Lebels thundered, deafening between the narrow walls.

The gray shadows came on, and went down, and came on again. No war cries there. Just the quiet working of bolts and the steady forward creeping which refused to be stemmed.

A bullet slammed into the machine gun and upset it. Reilly pulled it back on its legs and let drive once more. The belt ran out. Reilly fumbled behind him, searching in the gunner's bandolier.

Gray ghosts rose up in a solid wall before him. A Berber's knife flashed bright cold fire as it came down. Reilly watched it come. His hands were tangled in the bandolier. He tried to stagger back. The chill arc was almost at its completion.

A French bayonet knifed up and missed. The butt cracked forward. The Berber screamed and jackknifed over his crushed chest. Morenz was still swearing.

Reilly heard an auto-rifle start upon his left. He ran to it. The gunner's white face was tense as he squinted through the indistinct sights.

"Give them a cross-fire!" bawled Reilly.

The gunner swerved the weapon without looking up. Reilly ran across to the other side. "Machine guns!" he cried.

Metal rattled toward him. A sweating Legionnaire slammed the tripod to the ground. Another jerked at a belt, which twisted like a maimed snake.

"Cross-fire!" said Reilly.

After that it was short and to the point. The Berbers out front were unable to find shelter from the converging streams of fire. Legion bayonets came up, flashing in the faint light. Somehow the bayonets were floating in the air. The Legionnaires themselves were invisible against the tan walls.

The gray shadows ran toward a far hillside. The Legion's machine guns clattered stridently. Three-five, eight-five bursts. Men fell. Even in this faint starlight it was impossible to miss.

Reilly's voice was hoarse. "Enough! Form fours!" The men shuffled into place. The machine gunners crouched over their squat weapons, making certain that the Berbers did not come back.

Morenz counted, and then turned to Reilly. "Forty-one, sir. Three wounded."

Reilly nodded. "Load the wounded on *cacolets*. We haven't any time to lose." He looked back at the girl, who had ridden up to the mouth of the pass.

The column swung out toward the railroad, slogging tiredly. The *cacolets* jostled their burdens, the machine guns clanked and the boots went up and down. But you couldn't watch the boots in the night. You looked up and saw the stars, and had the feeling that you were not moving at all.

Walking at the girl's stirrup, Reilly listened to the horse's hoofs. They marked out three syllables with undeniable clarity. *"Sil-ves-tre—Sil-ves-tre."* Over and over.

And the marching boots said, *"DeGrille. DeGrille."* He had it coming, thought Reilly. If anything happened to the railroad, then he and Silvestre and deGrille would have at least one thing in common. Indeed *la belle Légion* was a jealous lady. Still, there had been that gruesome hand. He glanced up and saw the girl's fingers on the reins and felt better. At least he hadn't let them maim *her*.

"Nine men," she was saying gently. "And three wounded. Was it worth the price, Lieutenant?"

"Sure," said Reilly, as cheerfully as possible. "They pay you to die in the Legion." He wasn't trying to be heroic. He was trying to reassure her. No use for a girl to have nine men's blood on her hands.

Reilly went on: "Abd el-Ulad has been asking for it, anyway. And if we didn't set down our foot, he'd try something else." In the silence that followed, the hoofs still said, *"Sil-ves-tre."* And the boots tromped out, *"DeGrille."*

21

"You're an American, aren't you?" she asked.

"I guess so. My mother was, and I lived in the US for a long time. My father—Lieutenant Edouard William deReilly is the name. Bill Reilly. I thought you were an Englishwoman."

"No. To the Riffs, all white women are English. And, naturally, 'Christian dogs.' They wouldn't touch a Christian with their djellabas, unless it was for the purpose of making him uncomfortable."

"I know," said Reilly. "What happened to the others?"

"Their guns," she said quietly, "were too attractive and their horses too good. We were attacked far back in the Atlas. They're all dead—the others."

"What were you?" said Reilly.

"A sort of traveling catalogue and stenographer. We were doing anthropological work, and I kept the notes."

"Dangerous to go back, wasn't it?"

"We found that out."

"And your husband—?"

"I'm not married."

"I'm sorry," said Reilly. "I didn't mean to pry into your affairs. It isn't any of my business."

"You mean you're sorry I'm not married?"

A Legionnaire laughed in the ranks. Realizing that Reilly might use that as an excuse to extract twice their present speed, the sound was cut off in midair, as though by a knife.

The hoofs went on with their monotonous word, and the boots slogged on across the dusty plain. Drugged by the sounds, the men were scarcely aware of the fact that they were near the railroad. Then they realized they were close. Within two kilometers.

The shrill whistle of the engine drifted to them faintly. They could see that dot of yellow which was the headlight, and they could hear the undertone of banging wheels and rattling cars.

Reilly began to breathe more easily. Maybe everything was coming out all right after all. Maybe Abd el-Ulad hadn't had anything in mind but glory when he sent that challenge.

And then Reilly knew how wrong he was. The plain was ripped by shattering sound and livid fire. The harsh crunch of telescoped steel came to them plainly. They swung into a fast double time. Reilly held his breath.

Immediately following the explosion there came a concerted yell. Rifles hammered. By the light of the burning train they could see the swirling djellabas of the Riffs.

Men were running across the plain. They were Spaniards, cut down by rapid volleys before they could reach cover. Riffs swarmed over the derailed cars, looting and killing.

Reilly found breath enough to bellow an order. The Legionnaires swung out into fan formation and charged.

But they were too late, too far away. The Riffs heard them come and did not pause to shoot. Their work was finished. A regiment of Spanish soldiers lay scattered and lifeless on the weirdly lit plain. A thousand rifles and hundreds of cases of ammunition were already being carried at breakneck speed toward the lines of Abd el-Krim.

Reilly drew up. Everything was silent now, except for the bright crackle of the fire. His adjutant, left on guard with a squad, came out to him and walked beside him.

"I couldn't hold them off!" exclaimed the adjutant. "They drove us in the—"

Reilly waved him away and sank down on the edge of the platform, staring with dull eyes at the carnage.

The girl dismounted and started to approach him. Then, her mouth tight and her eyes bright with tears, she went away toward Reilly's hut.

Reilly's hands hid his face. He could wipe away the sight of that burning train, but he could still hear the crackle. Silvestre and deGrille would soon have company. . . .

CHAPTER FOUR

The Legion Condemns

THE military tribunal was, to Reilly, a sea of grave faces and gold braid. Standing out in the center of the whitewashed room, he felt very much alone. Electric fans whirred, and flies buzzed in and out the open windows. Against the far wall stood a file of soldiers with fixed bayonets.

Colonel d'Avril, his chest blanketed by campaign ribbons, his mouth lost in a spiked gray beard, rolled a pencil between thumb and forefinger. He glanced at Reilly.

"Lieutenant," said d'Avril, "we deliberate too long and listen too much. I think it would be better if I were to state this matter in so many words and allow the judges to cast their ballots.

"You are charged, Lieutenant deReilly, with having deserted your post under fire. None of this talk about women in distress or the compulsion of chivalry is pertinent.

"Through that desertion, Lieutenant, some hundreds of Spanish soldiers lost their lives. Had you remained on duty, this would not have occurred.

"In more ways than one, Lieutenant, you made a military error. You should have known that this was a mere trick to throw us off the railroad. Abd el-Krim is clever, and should he find that our army is made up of men no quicker-witted than

25

yourself, it will be impossible for France not to be embroiled in the conflict between the Riffs and Spain.

"Thus, by disobedience of orders, Lieutenant, you have precipitated a grave crisis. It is your fault that we are here instead of at the coast fighting to retain control of France's rightful possessions.

"My summation, Lieutenant, is simple and to the point. You *did* desert your post in face of fire. You admit it. All else is irrelevant.

"Sergeant! Return the lieutenant to his quarters."

Reilly's haggard face shifted as he looked at the remaining judges. He saw there nothing but scowls. He about-faced and walked to the entrance, soldiers closing in on each side.

People drew hurriedly away from the door to let him pass. The blinding sunlight fell hot and dry against the back of his dress blues. The boots of the Legionnaires rang sullenly as they crossed the court to Reilly's quarters.

Two sentries paused at the steps and dropped their rifles to order arms. The others went away.

Reilly walked along the veranda without seeing anything. His eyes were blank, his mind was dull, his head ached. More than anything else he wanted a cigarette.

He wasn't thinking that this was the end of his career. He wasn't thinking that he would be lucky to get off with a light prison sentence. He thought not at all. During this past fortnight, his brain had become weary of speculation.

A cigarette was in his hand. He did not question its source. He fumbled for a match, and then a match was there. The taste of the smoke brought him back a little. It was American, that cigarette, and it tasted good after Algerian tobacco.

Turning, he saw the girl for the first time since his arrest. She was dressed in a cool, thin print. Her smile was a little tremulous, as though she wanted to stay, but found that the application of the wish took courage.

"What's—happening?" she faltered.

His voice was rough, his eyes were two black diamonds. "They're deciding now, Miss MacArthur. Thank you very much for the cigarette." He started to walk away, but she caught the braided sleeve of his tunic.

"No, don't go. I came to— Lieutenant, I've been trying for two weeks to pull wires for you. I have money, too much of it. But they won't listen to me. They don't want my money. I've told them and told them and told them that it was *my* fault, that I should take the blame. But—but they won't listen."

He turned again. "I thought you'd forgotten."

"How could I? After all I've done to you in payment for what you did for me— Lieutenant, you must believe me."

"You can drop the 'lieutenant,' Miss MacArthur. The name is Reilly. Bill Reilly. Prisoner umpteen thousand umpteen."

"Don't be bitter."

"I'm not. Don't let it worry you. I'm not sorry for what I did. What do I care for Spain? You're worth more to—you're worth more than all the people in this festering country, so don't think I'm angry at you or at anything. I've had my run of luck, and the sand is out of the glass. It's all through, and I'm through. Maybe if they just send me to prison, instead of before a firing squad, I can start over again—somewhere."

"I'll stay by you, Bill Reilly." Something in the way she said it made him face her squarely.

He placed his hands on her shoulders and looked into her eyes. "Now listen. Please don't take this thing to heart. You don't have to stay by me. In fact, you can't. Go back to the United States and forget it. Take the next boat. This country almost got you once. Don't let it have another chance. You *will* go, won't you? For me?"

"No," she said, averting her eyes.

"But you must listen!"

"I'm staying by you."

"Please, Miss MacArthur! You're borrowing grief and trouble. You can't—"

He was startled at the expression on her face. He had not known she could look like that.

"You can't change things, Bill Reilly. Not now, you can't. It's too late, I tell you. Much too late. When you walked into that hut and turned me free, when you blasted your way through that pass—" Her head went down and she stared, unseeing, at the floor.

With an electric shock he knew what she was driving at. She wasn't saying all those things from a sense of duty. She—

The sergeant had come back. Reilly fell in between the files and they marched to the tribunal through the withering heat.

When he once more stood alone in the center of the room, Reilly saw that the colonel had a stack of slips before him.

The colonel's tone was impersonal, almost disinterested.

"You are sentenced," he said, "to fifteen years with the *bataillon pénal*."

The desks wavered before Reilly's eyes. They couldn't—that was impossible. He was an officer, not a Legion private. Fifteen years—when five years was considered equal to the death penalty!

He saluted with a steady hand. *"Oui, mon Colonel,"* he said. He about-faced and found himself again in the file of fixed bayonets. They were not marching to his quarters this time. They were on their way to the cells.

The colonel's voice became a mere whisper behind him. But he heard the colonel say, "—make an example of him. That's what the service needs. No discipline. All medals and parades. This ought to . . ."

CHAPTER FIVE

"Got Himself Fifteen Years!"

THE cell was lined with slabs of wood which served as bunks. Countless generations of incarcerated Legionnaires had scrawled their brand of wit and defiance upon the stucco walls and had left an ample assortment of insects who cared nothing about their victim's rank.

Reilly had been given a block to himself, but from a nearby tier he heard muttering and singing and swearing—Legionnaires who would be restored to duty after they were sufficiently sober.

One high-pitched voice was calling across the corridor in French, "And he's an officer, so help me! Got himself fifteen years with the Zephyrs!"

"They can't do that to an officer," came a rumbled reply. "Of a surety they can't—and yet there he is."

"What was it all about?"

"Got himself all tangled up with some skirt, I hear. Made a monkey out of him, she did. She was a spy from Abd el-Krim, and she made him steal the plans of Meknes."

"Aw, you're all wrong!" objected still a third party. "She was a Spanish dame that the Spaniards sent over here to find out the way the French stood on the Riffian idea. And when she found out that France was staying out of it, she tried her best to get them into the scrap. And then this lieutenant, because

31

he loved her so damn much, tried to start the Riffs and the French scrapping. It's as plain—"

"Shut up!" said an evident non-com. "He can hear you!"

Reilly drew his arms around his knees and stared at the square of light that came from the high window. Yes, he could hear them, and it wasn't helping any. Fifteen years in the *bataillon pénal*. . . .

The first to speak was at it again. "Bet he won't love her so much now. Fifteen years in the Zephyrs. Fifteen years of marching around in circles, with a seventy-pound bag of sand on a regular marching pack—"

"Fifteen years! Yeah? They don't last any fifteen years. I remember the time Phelps went down there for knifin' that captain. They sent him in for five years. The poor guy didn't last two. They drilled him eight hours a day, and made him sleep outside, with no blankets, in a corral. And then when he died, they just threw his carcass in a lime pit and let it go at that. Fifteen years? He won't last three!"

"Three? I'll bet he lasts more than that! He's Bill Reilly, that's who he is!"

The talking died to a mutter. The name went the rounds. Bill Reilly? Sure, Bill Reilly. Didn't know he was even up here. Thought they sent him back. He's too tough to kill, Zephyrs or no Zephyrs. Remember the time down at— How'd *he* let himself get— Anybody'd fall for a Spanish dame. . . .

Reilly's black eyes still stared at the yellow square. His hair was rumpled and his uniform was hanging loosely from his shoulders. Hanging loosely because the buttons were gone, hacked off. His sword was still out there on the parade ground, in two bright pieces.

They were talking again, they had forgotten about him.

"I'll bet you," said a throaty German voice, "that we're in it in three months."

"Make it two weeks. The Riffs are raising hell with us. They murdered two patrols that weren't even trying to fight. That guy Skim—"

"Krim—Abd el-Krim. They're calling him Our Lord up there. He's got two cities under siege, and he's bringing every man in the Riff under his flag. They'll wipe out the Spanish all right. Never thought a Spanish a good fighter, anyway."

"I heard," said another, "that we were helping the Riffians. How about that? That don't look like we're going into war with them, does it? Hardly!"

"Aw, who the hell told you anything like that? You're crazy."

"S'truth. I got it straight from an intelligence runner. He was standing in the tent and—"

"If you got it from Intelligence, you'd better watch yourself. They'll make you scatter around pretty fast. Might even stand you against the wall. Intelligence isn't fooling with anybody these days."

"Lord, but I'd hate to be one of those guys. All they do is get bumped off. Saw one of them once. The Arabs had driven him into the sand, and then they'd left just his head showing. So they gouged out his eyes and ran their horses at him. He'd think he was about to get stamped on when they'd shear away. Pretty soon they left him, and the sand and sun cooked him brown. Just like a pork roast, I tell you. It's a suicide section, the Intelligence."

"Yeah—you're right. I'd rather be in the Zephyrs than in Intelligence. You can get out of the Zephyrs."

"Shut up—here's the sergeant!"

Reilly looked up at the yellow square and listened to the hammering of hobnailed boots coming down the corridor. They wouldn't be coming for him. He wasn't destined to get out for several days. And then it would be to board a train for Sidi-bel-Abbès and the *bataillon pénal.*

The square of light was blacked out. Maybe they were coming for him after all. A key grated harshly in the door and the sunlight flooded the place, blinding him.

The sergeant said, "Four minutes, that's all. I'll be waiting outside."

The door closed again and Reilly opened his eyes. He shook his head. He was seeing things, going crazy. But no—maybe he wasn't. She was close to him. She even placed her hand on his sleeve.

Somebody in the next tier called out, "It's the dame!"

"Why did you come?" said Reilly in a low voice.

"I came—" He couldn't see her face so well. "I came because I had to tell you goodbye."

"Then you're leaving for the US?"

"Yes. I'm leaving, but I'll come back. However long it may be, I'll come back. Oh, why—?"

"Don't," he said gently. "Don't make it tough for yourself. I'll get along all right. I always have."

"But I don't want to *leave* you!"

The sergeant said, "Four minutes, that's all.
I'll be waiting outside."

"That can't be helped."

"I've spoken to the colonel about you. I've tried every way I know to do something for you, but I can't get anyone's attention. They all treat me as if I was an—an enemy of France. They won't let me do anything or say anything. And I want so much to stay by you! I can't let you go off all alone!"

"You'll have to," said Reilly.

"I thought for a while yesterday that I had the colonel's attention. He sat there rapping his desk with a pencil and staring at nothing, and I thought he was actually listening. But he wasn't. He turned around to me and I knew that he had just remembered that I was there. I'm so sorry, Bill!"

The sergeant cleared his throat outside. "Time's up, miss."

Reilly went to the door with her. The lock was rattling. Her hand was strong on his shoulder. Then the door opened and closed and she was gone.

Reilly went back to the bench.

"Don't blame him," called one Legionnaire to another. "Did you get a good look at her? Ooo-la-la!"

"What wouldn't I give to be in his boots, Zephyrs or no Zephyrs!"

"She wasn't any Spick. She was an American. I know 'em when I see 'em."

"Man, oh man! Think of having a dame like that over you! It's worth thirty years in the batallion for every tear. Those eyes—"

"Eyes! He was looking at her eyes!"

Reilly kicked the door. "You lousy camels! You fatherless

idiots! You misbegotten hogs! If you say one more word I'll kick down this door and strangle every damned mongrel in the place!"

After that there was silence. And dusk. And the call to colors, soft and sweetened by distance.

CHAPTER SIX

Suicide Mission

EVEN on the bled, it's cold in those ugly predawn hours, with a coldness that seeps like steel through the body. Misery is never greater than at three in the morning.

Reilly had been unable to sleep. He had sat with his knees drawn up to his chin, staring at a star. He thought it was Vega, but he was not sure. He could see the star, now that it had moved into the square of dark sky. By cocking his head a little on one side he could see another, but it was not so bright.

Snores came from the other tier. Those fellows had nothing to worry them. In a day or two they would be restored to duty, and a mark in a book already black is of little importance.

A pair of boots scraped on the gritty stone. Probably a non-com changing the guard. The boots came nearer, still gritty, hobnails scratching the pavement. Reilly, still watching the star, heard a key rasp. The star was blotted and Reilly felt slightly annoyed, for no good reason, except that the square had been moved.

"Come on out of there," said the shadow in the cell entrance. Reilly moved a little. The man reached forward and took Reilly's arm. Reilly did not know why he did it—perhaps because this fellow had taken away the star. His fist swooped through two feet of blackness and cracked solidly against the man's jaw.

With a sigh, the Legionnaire folded up across the wooden slabs.

Getting stiffly to his feet, Reilly eyed the prone body. It didn't immediately come to him that he was free, but when it did, he walked slowly to the door and looked out.

No lights, and no sounds. Just blue-white darkness and the whisper of chill wind across the bled. He looked about wonderingly.

He wanted to run, but he did not. He knew how little use running was. No place in Morocco would be safe. He couldn't hide from the Legion, and if he did, the Riffs would kill him. Silently he rolled the idea around his mind. No, it wouldn't be right.

Going back to the Legionnaire, he lifted him with one hand. He scooped water from a bucket by the wall, threw it into the man's face.

"Snap out of it," ordered Reilly.

Dazedly the Legionnaire came to. He blinked and backed up, thinking, no doubt, that he was about to receive his own bayonet in the stomach. Fumbling at his side, he saw the bayonet was still in its scabbard.

"Well, out with it. What do you want?"

The Legionnaire tried to look official, mobilizing his battered wits. "The colonel wishes to speak with you, sir."

"Lead away," said Reilly.

"After you, sir."

Reilly went out.

The breeze was colder and the buttonless coat flapped like

a scarecrow's jacket. Reilly's feet slogged tiredly through the dust.

A man was standing on the colonel's veranda, watching them come up. The man was dressed in breeches and shirt. An automatic was buckled under his armpit.

Reilly stopped, without saluting or coming to attention. This, oddly, was the colonel—and colonels are usually in bed at three AM.

"Good morning, Lieutenant," said the colonel. "Come in. Dismissed, soldier."

The guard went away, shaking his head and feeling of his doubtlessly smashed jaw, which was just beginning to hurt.

Mounting the steps, Reilly entered the front room of the colonel's quarters. A light burned there, unseen from the parade ground. The colonel's shadow was grotesque against the drawn blinds.

Reilly sat down, and the colonel pushed a bottle of cognac toward him. "Have a shot. Warm you up."

Eyes watchful, Reilly drank. He failed to understand what this call meant, but he was willing to stand by. Lighting one of the colonel's cigarettes, he took a deep drag and looked at the blinds, where the colonel's shadow moved.

"Lieutenant," said the colonel, "you're a doomed man. No one has ever lived through fifteen years of the *bataillon pénal*."

No answer was expected. Reilly watched the shadow.

"As I say, you're doomed. And through your own foolishness. But I must tell you, Reilly, that it was with a good deal of trouble that I had you convicted."

41

"Did you call me over to gloat, *mon Colonel*?"

"Here, have another drink—plenty of it here. As I say, Lieutenant, I had a good deal of trouble getting you convicted. You must have thought me terribly hard on you. The others did. They're incurable romantics, those others."

"Go on, *mon Colonel*."

"It was hard, Reilly, because I had a definite purpose in mind. A quite definite purpose." The colonel's eyes, in the light of the single lamp, were colorless. His wedge-shaped head was cocked to one side.

"You, Lieutenant, were discharged from the service, kicked out, had your sword broken on parade."

"Yes," said Reilly. "A beautiful show."

"Precisely, Lieutenant. A show—and nothing *but* a show. There are eyes that see all we do and tongues that carry those actions to ears that can use them. You, Reilly, are a doomed man—*in the eyes of Abd el-Krim!*"

Reilly sat up. "Intelligence?"

"Intelligence, Lieutenant. You are now one of that unsung band of heroes who—"

"Save it. Send me to the *bataillon pénal,* but not to your Intelligence."

"You would rather die a criminal than a hero?"

Reilly poured himself another drink and stretched his legs out before him. His buttonless coat flapped from his shoulders. His eyes, over the glass rim, were hard black diamonds.

"There isn't any use bucking you, *mon Colonel.* You have decided that I must die a hero, and a hero I will die."

Colonel d'Avril rubbed his hands and stood up. His shadow

quivered on the blind. He took two restless paces down the center of the room and then came back.

"Lieutenant, you do not think France is in this Riffian war. You think France is striving to stay neutral."

"I thought so. That was the basis of your trial."

"A blind, Lieutenant. Have you looked at the maps of Morocco? I know that you have. Do you remember the division of land between the Spanish and the French? Lieutenant, the French have entirely too little of that territory. We need it as a dying man needs the blood he has spilt. Spain has cut our throats. They want all Morocco. And they are battling the Riffs."

"Go on," said Reilly, drinking slowly.

"The situation is this. The Riffians are hammering the Spanish with every ounce of the Riffian manpower and resources. And the Riffian is gradually becoming drained of both. Soon, Lieutenant, they will be weak."

"And easily whipped."

"Precisely. And Spain is breaking its spine trying to stave off those attacks. Lieutenant, we shall see Spain driven into the sea. And we shall see France wiping out the Riffians—*after* the Riffians have served our purpose."

"Purpose?"

"Yes. The Riffians need guns, and bullets and modern weapons. They need things we can give them. Given these things, the Riffians will whip Spain."

Reilly listened to the throb of excitement in the colonel's voice.

"And then," whispered d'Avril, "we will beat down the

Riffians, when their strength is gone and when the Spaniards have been cast aside."

"They'll fight with our weapons," said Reilly.

"It is no matter. They will be soon tired of war."

"Where do I come in?"

D'Avril chuckled. "That is the clever part. You escape. You go to Abd el-Krim. You tell him that France has cast you out. He will believe you, because your disgrace was witnessed by his own agents. He will give you a free rein, and you will use it."

"How?"

"We will ship munitions to Spain. But you will know when they are shipped, and what country they will traverse. And you, at the head of a flying column of Riffians, will capture these arms for distribution among the men of Abd el-Krim."

"What about search for me?"

"I will try to block that."

"What about my possible capture by French troops?"

"That will be taken care of—perhaps."

"What if I should fall into Spanish hands?"

"They would torture you. It has to be chanced."

"What happens if Abd el-Krim fails to believe me and has me killed?"

"That, too, must be chanced. No one must know of this, Lieutenant."

"And if I get free, and this is done?"

"Perhaps," said d'Avril, "France will help you get out of Africa. Perhaps, before long, I shall be a general of France."

"But you promise nothing."

"Lieutenant, like yourself I am only a cog in a military machine. Matters such as you mentioned are not in my control. I have my orders, and you have yours. There is the door, Lieutenant, and here on the table lies a brace of revolvers. I send an Intelligence man with you."

Reilly stood up and poured himself another drink, his black eyes reckless. Raising it, he held it toward the sea. "Here's to Krim and the Suicide Section."

A hooded figure was at the door mounted on one horse, holding another. Reilly thrust the revolvers into his belt and strode out to the barbs. Swinging up, he bent from the saddle in a brief, mocking bow.

"Until we meet again, *mon Colonel*."

Hoofs spurned sand, and the fading cold night blotted the riders from sight.

The colonel listened long to the retreating sound of steel on sand. Then he turned into the house and brushed his brow with a shaking hand.

"'Until we meet again!' *Mon Dieu!* He thinks he can live through it!"

CHAPTER SEVEN

The Meeting with Abd el-Krim

F AR out across the bled, heading west, traveling with the morning sun hot against his back, rode Reilly. The fields were filled with burnt, withered stubble. A few weeks before, this had been a sea of marigolds, night-scented stock, blue iris and small wild orchids. The summer suns had taken these, leaving the bled a rolling tan wasteland.

The ever-present Atlas crawled to the south. Unless one studied them intently, it was impossible not to believe them a drifting bank of blue-white clouds. A haze cut them off from the earth, and the peaks, snow-clad even at this time of year, reared rugged heads into a blued steel sky.

Reilly paid little attention to his companion. Some Intelligence man, doubtless, who was there to see that he went through with the deal and who would desert to carry back a report as soon as the fighting became too thick. Intelligence men were far from cowards, but they had the unhappy faculty of putting France above mere human life, and they were apt to turn up missing when you needed them most.

The shaggy barbs plodded on, heads drooping sorrowfully in the blasting heat. Reilly stopped once and peeled off his tunic, lashing it to the cantle. It bothered him, flapping against his ribs. Each flap reminded him that it had no buttons.

He fell to wondering about d'Avril. The man had persisted in addressing him as lieutenant. Courtesy—or sarcasm? Cool lad, that d'Avril. His head was narrow like a wedge and his lips were thin behind his beard. His eyes were chilly, always looking into the far distance, as though eternally dreaming of empire.

They came, in the afternoon, to a deserted, muddy well. The surrounding soil was packed down by the feet of countless generations of alien camels and native horses. Here and there an elliptical print was visible. These would be made by gun butts. The party who had stopped here last had obviously been on their way to join Abd el-Krim.

Reilly swung down and drained his canteen. After filling it, he glanced up at his hooded companion, who had not dismounted.

"Drink?" said Reilly.

A shake of the head was all the answer he received. The detachment of this companion made Reilly frown.

After that they went on again across the burnt plain. The afternoon faded and the sun was in Reilly's eyes. Then the sun dived behind the mountains and left the sky a flaming sea of unbelievable color.

Reilly stopped and looked at the Atlas. Sometimes, he thought, this Morocco was almost worth living in. He watched the red fade into a deep purple, and then he saw the evening star hang out its lantern.

It was dark when they went on. To the right and left, from far across the bled, came lights. Cooking fires of the Berbers.

There were other lights ahead, a sparkling cluster made by flames on the side of a hill.

Reilly rode closer to the lights, watching his path. This must be a body of troops en route to another battleground. Only a large detachment would dare to light so many fires in enemy country.

In the shadows beside the trail, Reilly glimpsed a small red glow. His horse shied away. A sentry materialized out of nothing. He held an old Spanish Mauser, from the end of which projected a sharp bayonet.

"Dismount!" ordered the sentry in Shilha.

Reilly held the horse with one hand and swung easily down to face the Berber. His hands were far from the revolver butts. A gunshot would be classed as suicide.

"Ah," hissed the sentry. "A Spanish spy!"

"I'm French," replied Reilly in the man's dialect. "A deserter."

"They all claim that. Every one of them. You're Spanish, and a spy. I need no orders from Our Lord to know how to dispose of you."

"Your lord?"

"Abd el-Krim, you misbegotten camel! Our Lord, Abd el-Krim."

"Then he is here."

"Returning to Ajdir. You wish to know too much." The sentry shifted his footing.

The bayonet sparkled in the starlight as the man lunged. The blade swept toward Reilly, with all the Berber's weight behind it. Reilly's hands came up. One gripped the barrel, the other snapped to the stock. The steel-shod butt slapped out of the Berber's hands and rocketed up. Bone snapped as the metal crushed the sentry's jaw.

In the same movement, Reilly reversed the gun and slashed out with the bayonet. It held for an instant, and then came free. The sentry's throat was cut. He dropped heavily, blood rattling in his windpipes.

Reilly released the gun and reached quickly down to retrieve the turban and djellaba before they became smeared with blood. He had them in a moment and was in the act of putting them on when an exhausted sigh attracted his attention. He wheeled and looked up at his companion, who was swaying in the saddle, beginning to slip sideways to the ground. Reilly snatched at the falling body and eased it to earth.

"What the hell's wrong with you?" whispered Reilly. "I've got enough to—"

He pulled aside the turban and hood and immediately felt as though someone had picked him up and smashed him against a wall. It was unbelievable, but the evidence was right there before him.

Kay MacArthur's quiet face lay upon his arm.

Roughly he shook her into consciousness. When her eyes flickered and when her body stiffened in his grasp, Reilly growled, "Now what the hell are you trying to do?"

Her dark eyes were pleading. "I had to come. I couldn't stay away from you."

"You know that I can't go back to the Legion and take you. You know that I'm classified as an escaped prisoner. I can't take care of you out here."

"Have I just succeeded in making things difficult for you again?"

"Yes."

She drew back from him. "I'm sorry I passed out. But all day without food, and with no water—" She looked down at the dead sentry, whose head was twisted at an impossible angle. The sentry's cigarette still burned in the sand.

"I offered you water at that well," he reminded her.

"I know, but we were still close to headquarters and I thought if I took off the hood to drink you'd recognize me and take me back."

"Don't talk," he breathed.

The slow movements of a squad of men came to them faintly.

"If I'm found here with this corpse—" said Reilly angrily. He pushed her away from him and adjusted turban and djellaba about his head and shoulders.

Taking the shoulders of the sentry, Reilly pulled him back under the shrub out of sight. He tried to scatter sand over the dark pool of blood, but the blot persisted in coming through.

He came back to Kay. "You little fool!" he began hotly. Then he saw her face, soft and beautiful in the starlight. His inflection changed. "You little fool!" He reached out and crushed her against him, running his fingers through her silken hair.

The tramp of marching men was louder. Reilly pulled the girl's hood over her head and turned just in time to see the first of the patrol.

The Berber stopped, his white face tense. His gray eyes glowed strangely in the half-light. "Who are you?"

Reilly gave him a smile and a short bow. "If it pleases you," he replied in Shilha, "I come with a message for Our Lord."

The Berber thrust a finger at the bloody sand. "And what is this?"

Reilly's tone was insolent. "One of your sentries. You should teach these Arabs better manners before they are allowed to fight with Berbers."

The other's face relaxed. Arabs and Berbers are not exactly bosom friends. "An Arab, was he? Then nothing is lost. But—" He stared keenly at Kay. "I must arrest you and take you to Our Lord. He attends to justice here."

Two other Berbers grasped the reins, and a file closed in around Reilly and the girl. They walked toward the fires.

Men were squatting on their heels about the flames, roasting cubes of meat spitted upon their knives and bayonets—kabobs. They looked up curiously, then went on eating.

Noticing the girl's frightened glances to the left and right, Reilly sought to distract her attention.

"How did you manage this?" he asked.

She smiled a little. "It was not too hard. I paid d'Avril a thousand dollars when I found out what he intended to do with you. One woman, more or less, means very little to d'Avril, compared to France—or a thousand dollars."

A large tent was looming up in the light of the fires that flanked it. From the interior came a flickering light. Reilly was forced to stop while the "sergeant of the guard" entered.

In a moment the "sergeant" was back, motioning for

both Reilly and Kay to enter. They found themselves in a low-ceilinged, canvas-partitioned room. By the sputter of a wick in a cup of fat, a thickset man was thumbing through sheafs of orders. When he glanced up, Reilly saw an intense and burning fire in the eyes.

"My Lord," said Reilly in Shilha, "I have come to offer you my services."

"That is simple. Why do you bother me? See one of my captains and receive an issue of rifle and ammunition—I am too busy."

Reilly bowed. "May I undeceive you, My Lord? I am neither a Berber nor an Arab. I am Lieutenant Edouard William deReilly, formerly of the French Foreign Legion."

Abd el-Krim sprang up. The surprise died out of his face and he tugged thoughtfully at his beard. "DeReilly, is it? Lieutenant deReilly, formerly of *la Légion.* And why, Lieutenant, do you come to me disguised as a Berber?"

"Because I fear the nervous trigger fingers of your men when they see a khaki uniform."

Abd el-Krim's intense eyes studied Reilly's face. "But . . . but I can do nothing for you! I could not trust you with any of my men. I have had to shoot two Legion sergeants who deserted and tried to help me drill my troops. I think it best, Lieutenant, that I oversee your immediate execution." He slapped his hand against the table and a guard bobbed through the entrance.

"Wait," said Reilly, his face very calm. "I bring with me a woman. A white woman."

"What do I care about that?"

"I did not expect you to care. It was she who caused the trouble with *la Légion* and me. And a very short time ago, I was sentenced to fifteen years in the *bataillon pénal.* Last night she effected my escape."

"You are trying to tell me what I already know," said Abd el-Krim. "But I am not at war with France, I am at war with Spain. Therefore, why do you seek vengeance through me against France?"

"Dismiss the guard," said Reilly.

Abd el-Krim motioned with his hand. "Wait outside. I will have need for you presently."

Kay threw back her hood and watched with alert, restless eyes. Krim paid her no attention.

"My Lord," continued Reilly, "I have a plan by which both you and I can profit. Vastly."

"And that plan?" Krim sank into a chair, leaning forward.

"You need the supplies of war. I can get them for you. It will be very simple. You pay me by the trainload."

"Where do these supplies—?"

"From French garrisons. It is very simple. I know the trains and their methods of guarding. I know what they will carry. They are shifting arms all over Morocco. I can keep your troops amply supplied with guns and ammunition—and even other things."

"How much a trainload?"

"Five thousand dollars."

"Too much."

Reilly smiled. "Name the price."

"Two thousand."

"Three thousand, five hundred—and the bargain is done."

Krim jerked his head in agreement. "Excellent! I know about you, deReilly. I know you were disgraced, and I believe you. You are Captain of One Hundred."

"Cavalry," said Reilly.

"Captain of One Hundred Cavalry, then. And you will be paid upon the delivery of the arms."

"In gold notes."

"In gold. Now go—I am very busy. We move onward tomorrow. I will have them give you a tent for this woman and yourself."

"Two tents," said Reilly.

"Two tents, then. Wait, before you go. I shall detail a man to watch you closely. If you try to communicate with either the French or the Spanish, giving them intelligence about my operations, I will have you shot. No, I will have your woman shot. Your head I will send to the French for a *petite souvenir.* That is all. Good evening."

They went outside and stood looking at the untidy camp while men procured their tents and food and clothing.

"Are you really—really going to attack French trains?" said Kay.

"I'm really going to attack French trains. And unfortunately, you will have to come along with me. I cannot leave you alone."

She touched his arm, unsteadily. There was a break in her voice as she said, "I stay with you, Bill Reilly, no matter what you do, no matter what happens."

CHAPTER EIGHT

Stark Betrayal

THE rain came early in the fall, out of season. The summer-dried land drank greedily of water, and grass was once more green. In the rolling hills a few miles from Fez, the French stronghold, flowers were beginning to bloom out of time. Far up in the Atlas it was snowing, and the white blanket stretched downward toward the foothills, calling attention to the fact that an early winter was not far away.

Abd el-Krim's men were restless. They had their wheat to reap and their winter food to store. And the war went on. The year before, they had deserted in droves just when the Riffs had the last of the Spaniards pinned in the citadel of the seaport of Melilla. The following spring had found the Spaniards reinforced, and the work of carrying on the *Jihad*—holy war—had to be done again.

Abd el-Krim had vowed that it would not happen twice, and so wheat rotted in the fields and deserters were shot in companies. The tide of the war had swung back and forth through the summer. Men were sickened by it, tired of fighting. Even the rapacious appetites of the Riffs were appeased.

The Spaniards were still there, holding on with gritted teeth, decimated and starved, ill-equipped, badly generaled. The Riffs, fighting in their own country, were better off for food and better off for weapons—thanks to some strange source of supply which could not be traced. Rumors were many. Some said that Abd el-Krim had started hidden factories of his own. Others stated baldly that the French supplied the weapons. Still others told a spine-tingling story of a mad Legionnaire who sold guns to Abd el-Krim by the trainload at so much a load. These added that the madman was possessed of black eyes, black hair and a voice like the horns of Ramadan.

There was also a rumor of a dark-eyed *Franzawi* girl always seen with the mad Legionnaire. One man told of the strange relationship which existed between these two. No one believed him, but of course it was interesting to hear that the mad Legionnaire never touched the girl, and that he had coldly shot down two men who had looked at her with more than passing interest. Yes, it was a good story, but one knew Legionnaires and soldiers in general.

Reilly, lying at full length in the tall green grass, squinted through field glasses at the dwindling rails, which were cut from sight by the end of the pass.

At his hand rested a black box from which a T rose like a tombstone. Wires trailed away from the box into the grass, worming their way out of sight, to reappear at the railroad.

A lynx-eyed Berber, Si Umzien, lay beside Reilly. "Do you see the smoke?"

"No, not yet. Do not be impatient."

"You call me impatient," said Si Umzien. "You have ranted all morning about the lateness of the train!"

Reilly took his eyes from the glasses and stared a hole through Si Umzien. The Berber subsided and turned over on his side to look up toward a fringe of trees.

"The lady, *sīdī*, is not keeping out of sight."

Reilly turned and looked up at the trees. Kay was leaning against a trunk, looking down at the valley and the rails. A silk djellaba flowed away from her shoulders to her Moroccan red boots. The yellow turban, swathed aslant about her head, was very bright—an excellent target. The white silk, baggy-sleeved shirt was bound in tight against her waist by a broad red sash—which was also a good target.

"Kay!" called Reilly. "Get out of sight! They'll spot you from the train!"

A murmur of assent went up from the crumpled grass, where some eighty men lay concealed.

Kay walked down to Reilly and dropped on her knees beside him. "It was cold among the trees. I'm sorry. This has become so common, I forgot there is danger."

"You never can tell," said Reilly, turning to the glasses. "Some sniper across the valley might think he needed to warm his gun." He grinned suddenly. "We've come through this far—don't let anything happen now."

Si Umzien's face was alight. "Are you going to blow up the engine this time, *sīdī*?"

"No."

"You never blow up the engine!" There was disappointment in his voice.

"I have to send them along," said Reilly. "And besides, as

I've said before, I don't like to blow up engines. It reminds me of something I try hard enough to forget."

Si Umzien shrugged. "Just so there is loot, *sīdī*." He remained silent for a moment. "They always amaze me, these forays. You try not to kill the *Franzawi*, and you let them escape. And the trains continue to come out of Fez loaded down with ammunition and guns."

"Always?"

"Well, not always. There were the four or five times the soldiers on the trains fought, and that other time a detachment of Spanish killed half of us before we killed them."

"We are not at war with France," said Reilly. "Abd el-Krim does not want me to kill the *Franzawi*."

"Our Lord is hard to please," said Si Umzien.

"Shut up, little ape!" hissed Reilly. "There comes the train!"

All eyes swept to the end of the valley, from whence came a curling column of greasy smoke. A whistle shrilled in a cloud of white steam, the sound reaching the slope after the steam was gone.

The engine and the lurching cars rolled out of the pass like an excited black snake, and charged across the valley, rattling and puffing importantly.

"Blow up the engine," pleaded Si Umzien. "Just this once!"

But Reilly had good reasons for avoiding that. And furthermore, he did not want to tear up the rails, as that would mean a delay. His hand went to the T on the black box. Kay watched with wide eyes and held breath. The eighty men did not move. They were silent.

The T came down. The tracks erupted in quantities of cinders and gray smoke. The train seemed to lean backward in its hurried attempt to stop before it reached the masking fumes.

Brakes screamed. Wheels yowled on the rails. The fireman leaned far out, staring anxiously.

"They'll stop in a minute and run," said Si Umzien. "They always do, and we never get in a shot."

The train stopped. The box cars and coaches disgorged a flashing array of steel and uniforms. And nobody ran.

Something was wrong, terribly wrong. Reilly pried himself off the ground and stared. Those men down there— He trained his glasses upon them. A machine gun tumbled out of a coach and was immediately set upon its tripod. A man was slinging a musette full of grenades over his shoulder.

"They're Senegalese!" cried Reilly.

The eighty men exhaled suddenly. Their voices were a rumbling mutter behind Reilly. The black troops of France were swinging into a skirmish line alongside the train. An officer was pointing up the slope, his voice lost in distance. The faint clamor of his whistle barely reached the Berbers. The skirmish line began to move, a line of gleaming black skin, bared teeth and red pants.

The machine gun clattered. The grass swished as bullets sped near Reilly's men.

"Machine guns!" cried Si Umzien. "Set up the machine guns. They'll be here—"

"Shut up!" snapped Reilly. "There's something wrong.

Don't shoot at them. Something's happened. There aren't any guns aboard that train except the guns those Senegalese are carrying."

Kay's face was white as she stared up at Reilly. "Get down! They'll kill you!"

"No!" Reilly whipped a piece of green cloth out of his pocket and started forward, unarmed, toward the advancing line, which had now reached the base of the slope.

The green flag cracked in the wind. In Berber country, green is the color of truce. Reilly watched, his black eyes alert. They weren't stopping, those Senegalese. They were coming on, and the officer who came first had already seen the flag. But the officer gave no order to stem the advance. There were fully five hundred men down there.

"Machine guns!" Si Umzien was wailing.

Reilly turned. "Don't fire on them. Wait. I'll give the signal."

Kay was calling to him. "Come back! They don't want to see that flag. You've been double-crossed!"

Standing there in his white, red-lined cloak, Reilly fanned the flag again. Certainly they'd come to a halt and parley with him! Surely that officer had orders! Reilly would hate to shoot even black soldiers, if they wore the uniform of France.

The machine guns were coming closer. A gunner planted his weapon at the foot of the hill and dropped on his belly behind the sights. The muzzle flashed white in a continuous stream.

Something tore at Reilly's side. He was flung around. Another leaden fist slammed him into the trampled green grass. The wave came on.

A Mauser roared. The spiteful bark of a Snider joined it. Two machine guns manned by Berbers began to chatter.

"They've got our captain!" screamed Si Umzien. He propped himself on his elbow and dragged a Lebel from his side. Resting his arm and taking careful aim, he squeezed the trigger.

The officer leading the Senegalese tripped, half his head blown away. The blacks swept on and up, dropping, getting up, running again. The wave attack. Half continually on the move, half prone, covering their brothers.

The Berber guns went to work, clattering like mowing machines. Red pants faltered and melted from sight. Si Umzien was taking toll with a calm hand, counting his cartridges and his late targets.

Kay tried to get to her feet. Almost without pausing in his marksmanship, Si Umzien knocked her back into the grass. He went on firing and counting.

The Berbers lay unstirring. The waves came up and went down. Senegalese toiled toward the crest, lips drawn back with effort. They flexed their arms, and their bayonets shivered. Gunfire was not for the black soldier. Knives were to his liking. Many had dropped their rifles to wave their own blade on high.

The Berbers leveled chill blue eyes across sights and sniped with a steadiness that made Kay shiver. The black soldiers were almost to the crest. Kay wanted to run, but could not.

She watched the flashing knives grow large. She saw the thick features of the men. She saw their tunics and their ribbons and their red pants. Through the smoke-thickened air they came on.

Si Umzien pressed a revolver into her hand, shouting to be heard above the tumult of guns. "Save one for yourself. These Senegalese are cattle. They torture the wounded. And women—" He went on shooting just as calmly as though he might not die in the next five seconds.

Kay couldn't shoot. Her hand was shaking. She looked through tear-dimmed eyes at the place where Reilly had gone down. The first wave had almost reached the spot. Her throat was hot, and the taste of the smokeless powder gagged her.

A blond-bearded Riff slammed a third machine gun down on Kay's left. He pushed the belt into her hand. "Feed it!" he roared.

Sitting up, she held the belt. Its snaky length was devoured by the breech. Smoking empties hurled back in a blurred arc of shining brass. The belt went on through. The Berber was squinting easily through the high sight, holding the jumpy barrel down with white-knuckled hands.

Kay found a second belt and thrust it out. A quick flip of the loading handle, and the gun went on. Kay did not dare look toward the slope. She was afraid of what she would see. It would do no good to look. If she should fall under a knife, it would be better not to know beforehand.

Si Umzien cried, "They're flanking us! Take that side!"

The gunner swiveled his piece and began to hammer at red blobs which were sprinting straight across the slope. Kay remembered hearing Reilly say, "When they run, lead them by half the width of their bodies." She wanted to tell the gunner that, but the crackling blast from the muzzle made it impossible.

Something attracted her attention on her right. She caught red cloth coming at her and the flicker of a red-stained blade. She screamed. Si Umzien turned and fired once. The Senegalese fell three feet from her, blood gushing from his nostrils and mouth. It smelled hot and salty.

Kay scrambled back, away from him, even though she knew he could no longer harm her. Her eyes went back to the spot where Reilly had fallen. A soldier had paused there for an instant, bayonet slanted down.

The revolver in Kay's hand exploded. The black soldier twisted about, dropping the rifle. The revolver fired a second time. The man was hammered back, falling as he went down the slope.

Machine guns doubled their fire. Sniders and Mannlichers and Lebels blended in one vast roar. Kay, on her knees, stared at the fallen man. She had killed a man.

When she looked up again she saw that the slope was strewn with patches of red and black. Far down the hill men were running to the train. The machine guns went on.

The engine sent out a greasy mushroom of smoke. Soldiers swung up by the handholds and into the vestibules. The train began to back rapidly.

The soldiers were gone, leaving their dead and wounded behind them. The train had gone from whence it had come. A man was screaming in a cracked voice far down the hill.

The blue-eyed Berbers stood up, stretching themselves,

rubbing recoil-numbed shoulders, spitting the taste of powder through their blond beards. Some of them walked cautiously down the hill and began to drag the wounded up to the shade of the trees.

Kay, stumbling, went down to the place Reilly had fallen. He lay on his side, his eyes tightly closed, the red lining of his cloak stained black.

A hoarse sound came from between clenched teeth. "Kay? Is that you, Kay?"

She knelt beside him and lifted his head. His black eyes were dull with agony.

"Take me—get them to take me up to the—trees."

Two Berbers bore him along, very gently. They laid him down beside a trunk on grass splattered with moving shadows. It was cool there. Another man came up and thrust a drug into Reilly's mouth, bidding him to swallow. Si Umzien was tearing strips from the red-lined cloak.

"Not serious," said Si Umzien to Kay. "He'll be around in a minute or so." Iodine from Reilly's first-aid pack gurgled into the wound. "No bullet in there," said Si Umzien, pulling out his finger. "Went all the way through."

A few minutes later, Reilly's eyes were blinking. They were no longer dull.

"Are there any whites among the wounded?" he asked.

"One. A man shot in the thigh." Si Umzien went away. Presently he came back, carrying a young lieutenant over his shoulder. He set the man gently on the ground.

When the lieutenant looked at Reilly, his face went white

and his hands shook. "Reilly. It's you, Reilly! Oh, God, don't torture me!"

The tone the man employed made Reilly sit up straight. He winced and lay back, closing his eyes for a moment. When he opened them again he said, "Where did you get the idea that I would torture you?"

"It's well known," cried the officer. "We've heard about it. We know what you've been doing." A hardness came into his voice. "We know, you renegade!"

Si Umzien, who understood French, bristled. "Let me shoot him, Captain."

"No," said Reilly.

The coldness of the threat was jarring. Lying half on his side, his wounded leg stretched out, the man stared into Reilly's face.

"Tell me," said Reilly. "Why did this attack come off?"

"The Legion has had enough of your raids on their posts. They've had enough of your killings."

"I have never raided a post, nor have I ever killed a Legionnaire."

The officer snorted, then remembered himself and sank back, watching Si Umzien's holster.

"Tell me more," Reilly said. "What has happened to France?"

"Don't tell me you haven't heard!" replied the officer gratingly. "France has declared war on the Riffs. She has allied herself with Spain against this barbarian Abd el-Krim."

Reilly sighed weakly and motioned with his hand. "Take

him away. When he gets his wound attended, turn him loose. Don't kill him, in spite of his insults."

Kay knelt at Reilly's side with a cool drink of water.

He did not notice the glass. "Kay, this is something we had not anticipated. France was going to declare war on both Spain and the Riff. Now she is allied with Spain. That means but one thing."

"What?"

"France, and the Foreign Legion, have used me as an excuse to do this. It means but one thing. We have no place to turn. We can't escape. We'll have to fight on through. The Riffs are suspicious of us. Spain has offered rewards. And now France betrays me by sending troops, instead of a shipment of guns."

"What are you going to do?" She watched his face become a haggard gray.

"Do? What can I do? I can take the railroad and hold it. I can betray France, but—" A surge of pain shot through him. "I—I guess I might as well stay by the tricolor. I'll guard their railroad, and try to—"

"Si Umzien!" cried Kay. But Reilly's adjutant was nowhere in sight. She bathed Reilly's head with damp cloths until his eyes opened again.

His lips were very close to hers. He started to reach up and pull her down to him, and then stopped. He shook his head and quietly fell asleep.

CHAPTER NINE

The Second Slaughter

THE fall wore on and the crops rotted in the fields. The Berbers had forgotten that there ever had been a time without the *Jihad*. Tanks, planes, field guns—all these were thrown in against them. And they fought on. The French and the Spanish were warring side by side, and the Riffs, under the inflexible, if not always brilliant, leadership of Abd el-Krim, held out against both.

Countless companies of Riffs lay entrenched outside Fez, the great French inland town, ready to launch forth a sweeping attack. And with the loss of Fez would go the loss of all Morocco. Fez was the pulse of the country, and the Riffs waited only for word from Abd el-Krim to seize the city.

West of Fez, along a crawling twin thread of steel rails, Si Umzien sat in the ramshackle station beside a field telephone box.

His eyes were intent with listening.

Reilly paced the dirt floor, looking out across the rolling plains and the wasted wheat each time he turned at the window. Kay sat on a bench against the wall, shuffling through a sheaf of messages.

Si Umzien's eyes began to gleam. He nodded and then quietly replaced the receiver. "He is wise, Abd el-Krim. Wise with the wisdom given only to saints."

"What are the orders?" barked Reilly.

"He tells the captains outside Fez to wait for reinforcements. There may be more than a garrison in the city. There probably is—these accursed infidel *Franzawi* have unlimited men. But we have them bottled up. They cannot escape. And Abd el-Krim is despatching troops on this very railroad to reinforce the captains outside Fez."

"And the train will be through—?"

"At midnight, and the attack will be at—" Si Umzien stopped. "You look at me strangely, Captain."

Reilly's gaze was steady. "I do because I am about to send you away."

"Me away! What have I done?"

"Nothing. I am sending you and the hundred away."

Si Umzien climbed slowly to his feet. "This is odd, Captain. Can it be that—?"

"Perhaps it is," said Reilly. "You can ride within ten minutes. Tell Abd el-Krim that he did not buy my services as a soldier. He bought them as a gun thief. He has paid me well. The contract is over."

"And you are going to try for Fez?"

Kay shifted uncomfortably. She could feel the clash of wills between the two. Their eyes were embattled. Si Umzien's were the first to drop.

"I thought," said Si Umzien "that this—this was all settled. I have not liked being under the command of a Christian. It was nauseous. As a man, you are a good man. But you are a Christian. And—"

"Hand away from your belt!" cried Reilly, dodging.

Si Umzien's revolver roared. The slug whined off the wall. Reilly dived through the smoke and picked Si Umzien off his feet and threw him bodily through the entrance. Si Umzien's gun was steady in Reilly's palm.

"Take your men," cried Reilly, "and go back to Abd el-Krim. Get gone before I blow out your brains!"

Si Umzien climbed to his feet. His eyes were brittle with desire to kill. But he walked steadily to the row of tents and called out an order. Men came into the sunlight, looked at the station and then began to pack their equipment.

Reilly went back to the wall and reached under the counter. A machine gun and a box of cartridges came forth.

"Will they fight you?" asked Kay.

"Yes. They were my friends only so long as I served their cause. But now that they have seen what I intend to do, they hate me, because I am against their cause."

"But I thought they were your—our friends."

"War is an odd thing, Kay. Men have no friends unless they are on the same side, the same company, the same squad. Carry those two rifles to the roof, and be quick. The men won't leave. They're collecting their wits."

He struggled up the steep steps behind her, lugging the machine gun. Returning, he pulled up the box of cartridges. He set up the gun and looked about him. The roof was flat, Moorish in design, with a barricade around it.

"They're going," said Kay, pointing.

"Perhaps," replied Reilly. "But they'll be back—they or another company."

Reilly sat down on the tripod seat and wiped the bolt

carefully, freeing it of dust and grime which might mean a jam.

When they had gone on the roof, the sun had been warm, but as the afternoon progressed a chill wind swept down from the Atlas and made Kay drag the white silk cloak tightly about her shoulders.

The Atlas began to turn from white to old rose and from old rose to flaming crimson. The sun dipped, spinning into the west, hidden behind the ranges. A soft afterglow was upon the world. The High Atlas floated above Morocco like murky gray ghosts.

Kay drew closer to Reilly at the machine gun. When she touched his arm he jumped.

"What were you thinking about?" she said.

"Oh, nothing much. I was just wondering how I was going to get you out of this awful mess."

"You don't need to worry about me. I have no one since Abd el-Krim killed the—up there in the Atlas."

"It's still a mess," said Reilly.

"I sometimes wonder if it is, after all. I've been happy at times." She fell silent, easing closer to his side, looking up into his face. "I wonder what you think of me, Bill Reilly."

"Does it matter?"

"Don't be so coldblooded! Not tonight. I know, without your telling me, that this will be the last stand, that you're going to make a glorious sky-rocket and then go out in a shower of flame."

Reilly nodded and caressed the trips of the gun. "As long

as I'm here, and as long as this gun is in place, they won't try anything. There are exactly three sticks of dynamite in that box, and some flares. I'm going to blow up the rails. The reinforcements will never arrive at Fez. I know, you see, that Fez is usually garrisoned by two hundred and fifty men. It might be a few more now, but I don't think so. There are countless foreigners in the town and Abd el-Krim has been balked for so long that he would butcher every single man, woman and child."

"And when the reinforcements do reach this point," whispered Kay, a little dazed by the thought of it, "some two thousand armed Riffs will leap out and charge us. And—"

"Curtains," said Reilly. "It's all I can do. I've been sitting here working out your route to the coast. You won't be molested."

"My route?"

"Yes. You can get across the bled, I'm sure. And you can get by the French at Casablanca. I have about forty-eight thousand dollars in gold notes."

"I didn't know it amounted to that much."

"It does. Here, take them and get the horse I left in the baggage enclosure. That's an order."

She looked fixedly at the money he had received from Abd el-Krim. Slowly she pushed it back against him and looked up into his face. "Take it and keep it. I have no wish to leave you."

"It's suicide," said Reilly. "You'd better forget me and go."

"Bill—don't you love me just a little?"

He gripped her arm between fingers which failed to notice

how they hurt. Then the grip relaxed and he looked back across the plain, which was gradually lighting up under a half-moon.

"You'd better go," he said.

"I can't, really I can't. I brought this all upon you, and I can't desert you. I've tried to help, but you haven't let me. You've treated me decently, but always with a cold courtesy that hurt. Can't you—please can't you tell me—just once?"

Reilly climbed off the tripod seat and picked up the box of dynamite. Swiftly he said, "Watch the gun." Then he clattered down the steep stairs.

She saw him crouch beside the rails far down the track. A bright glow was cupped in his hands. Sparks flew when he dodged quickly away. He came up the stairs three at a time.

"Down!" And he threw himself at full length under the protection of the barricade.

The flash came first. Then the thunderous explosion. Gravel and stones whistled overhead like bullets. Debris pattered on the roof for an indeterminable time.

"Good," said Reilly, getting up. "It blew up the telephone."

"Can't we run for it now?"

"They'd repair the track when they reached the break. They've heard from Si Umzien by now, and they must have the materials. It wouldn't hold them up an hour."

He straddled the tripod once more. "Watch behind us—they may try to come in from that direction. Thank God for a moon!"

The hours went by slowly and silently. The great expanse of rolling country was deserted all about them. The warm moonlight flooded the bled.

Kay tried to stifle the hammering of her heart. Occasionally she glanced around and looked at Reilly. He was a motionless white figure against the sky. There was something about the set of his shoulders, the way he carried his head—she knew he'd go out in a blaze of fire. It was like him. Some of his wild recklessness infected her. She felt heavy, after that. No matter how the morning would find them. . . .

The train was there almost before they sighted it. It breathed fire from its stack, and its wheels spurned the rails as it lashed its string of cars on through the moonlight.

Reilly did not move. He fingered the triggers of the machine gun and waited. This was unreal, weird beyond conception. Here were no bands and no flags. Just a quiet pair of hands on the butt of a gun, waiting for the train to stop and disgorge its troops.

So certain was Reilly that Si Umzien had communicated with Abd el-Krim, he began to wonder whether or not the engineer had forgotten how to stop the train.

Kay touched his arm and pointed in the opposite direction. "Look!"

Reilly, unwilling to take his eyes from the approaching train, glanced hurriedly about. He saw red and white flashes in the direction of Fez.

"They're attacking anyway!" he cried. A swelling lump of disappointment clogged his throat. This was all so useless!

Those Riffs would sweep Fez out of existence in the hour, unless something else had happened.

The train was almost to the breach, and it still had not slowed. Reilly held his breath, waiting for the inevitable.

Abruptly the engine pitched to one side of the track, spitting ragged streaks of fire. The cars slammed off the rails into a jumble of trash. A screaming medley of cries bit the air. The last car jumped to one side, whirled and came down on its front trucks, to telescope in a great blare of rent steel and wood.

Reilly was too startled to move instantly. Kay's hands were against the barricade. The sight of her brought him to life.

"Get down!" he bellowed, but she did not seem to hear. Reaching forward across the gun, he grabbed her arm and threw her under the protection of the barricade.

Men were crawling out of the wreck, babbling.

In the flare of the burning engine and the fire-scorched wooden coaches, Reilly saw a face. Even at fifty yards he could not mistake it. He had seen the man in Adjir a month before. Had seen him and marked him for later identification.

It was Abd el-Ulad—the Berber who had wrecked that Spanish train and wrecked Reilly's career!

The machine gun began to jar. Men stared up and fought to get at their weapons. The spitting streak of powder-flame sprayed through a wide arc. Rifle fire instantly came into being. A wave of men dashed out of the protection of the last coach and sprinted toward the station.

Reilly's thumbs were hard on the triggers. His eyes were

steady through the sights. He couldn't miss, with moonlight and firelight to guide his shots.

The belt rattled and the machine gun jerked. Onrushing men crumpled into silent heaps before the flailing bullets. They formed, and came on again. Reilly blasted them into oblivion.

Another belt was in his hand. He caught a glimpse of Kay's tense face. He fired again. The gun was getting hot.

Maddened by anger and fear, thrust forward by their captains, the Riffs charged a third time across the open plain. Reilly hammered a steady stream into their ranks, thinned them, annihilated them. He was remembering that other night, and those Spanish troops, mowed down before they could even start to run.

Cries of men blended with the crackling inferno which had been a train. Abd el-Ulad hovered in the background, distinguished by a scarlet turban, his bearded mouth emitting a steady stream of orders. Each time Reilly directed his fire in that direction, he found that it was worse needed elsewhere.

The third wave was gone. Men disappeared out on the plain as they plunged into ravines and out of sight. Reilly glanced at the place where Abd el-Ulad had stood. The man was gone.

With no targets in sight, Reilly mopped his sweaty forehead and leaned over the gun, checking its mechanism. Kay's hands were shaking, her eyes lusterless.

Looking over his shoulder, Reilly saw that the flashes on

the horizon had grown more distinct. He could hear nothing, deadened as he was by the sound of his own gun.

"Will they come back?" asked Kay.

"Yes. They'll come back. They think they can get through if they wipe us out."

Time flowed slowly and the moon ascended higher in the sky. The crackling of the flames died to an intermittent sputter. The plain was strangely quiet. Reilly began to believe that the Riffs had gone. But he knew them of old. As long as they stood a single chance of destroying him, they would come back. Perhaps they were planning something else, some different method of attack.

Kay leaned back against the barricade and watched the other side of the platform. Her breathing had become quiet and her hands no longer shook. The sight of the carnage, thought Reilly, must have been horrible for her to witness.

A scratching sound came to him faintly. He stiffened, listening more intently. Someone was coming up the stairs!

Leaving the gun, he crept to the top step. Kay, sitting up straight, watched him.

A gun flashed in front of Reilly's face! Reilly lurched back. In a swirl of cloth, two men leaped at him. Reilly snatched a gun from his belt, firing in the same motion. The first Riff fell forward. The second fired again. Reilly, straightening unsteadily, shot the man's throat away.

"Look out!" Kay screamed.

A larger Riff was already at Reilly's throat, roaring in a mighty voice. Reilly tried to sidestep, but the hands clung. He was staring into the face of Abd el-Ulad!

Kay was at the gun. She knew little about its operation, but she pressed the triggers and held it down. Behind her, Reilly swayed in the grip of the man who had once captured Kay MacArthur.

Kay knew what to do, although her hands felt leaden and her mouth was dry. As long as she sprayed lead over the edge of the parapet, Reilly would have a chance. Otherwise, the Riffs would swarm up and end it in the blink of an eye.

Reilly was swearing. His hands found and held Abd el-Ulad's wrists, keeping them away from his throat. From Reilly's thigh ran a warm stream of blood, burbling out from the ragged wound he had received from the first Riff.

The leg would not hold him. He sank back against the parapet, out over space. The machine gun rattled down into the moon-drenched plain. Men who sought to gain the stairs fell back and ran. The bullets were taking no effect, but to the Riffs, the sound was synonymous with death.

Reilly held on as long as he could. It was over twenty feet down to the wooden platform. The wound in his thigh had been numb, but now it began to send spasms of pain through him.

Abd el-Ulad's face was a grinning blur above him. The scarlet turban was like a pool of blood against the sky. Abd el-Ulad released one hand. The hand came back with a knife.

Reilly tried to knock the blade aside. The Riff's thumb pressed into his windpipe. Reilly swore with the last of his breath. He felt weak, utterly at the mercy of this man.

The knife ripped into his side in a flash of white pain. He tore away from the pressing thumb. Emptiness tugged at him. He turned over through space, and as he went, he could still see that patch of blood against the stars.

He scarcely felt the shock of striking the ground. Blackness came over him in nauseating waves, pulling him into a sticky mire which it was impossible to deny. He could still hear the machine gun. A new sound penetrated his consciousness. The sound of a train coming from the direction of Fez. Kay, then, wouldn't get away in time. Kay . . .

Kay heard Reilly's last curse. She swung about and stared across the flat roof at Abd el-Ulad. The man was turning to her, turning slowly as though he possessed an eternity of time.

Abd el-Ulad's voice barely reached her ears. "We meet again, Miss MacArthur. But, unfortunately, this time I have no use at all for you. And so—" He shrugged and walked toward her, pulling a pistol from his belt.

Her eyes were wide with terror. "Stop!"

Abd el-Ulad chuckled. "It is like killing a little goat, but you have done too much to be spared. It is too bad, but—" His thumb drew back the hammer and he raised the muzzle.

It seemed an interminable time before the hammer clicked at full cock. She heard the rushing of a train somewhere near them, coming toward them. It was still far away, and it would bear more Riffs, victorious after the sacking of Fez. She regretted in that moment that the light of the still burning wreck would show them that the track was closed.

As if from a far distance she heard a rattling cough. She had heard that sound before when men had died. It would be . . . Her eyes grew wider. A surge of hate ran through her.

*"We meet again, Miss MacArthur. But, unfortunately, this time
I have no use at all for you. And so—" He shrugged and
walked toward her, pulling a pistol from his belt.*

The night turned red before her eyes. She had suddenly realized that this Riff, Abd el-Ulad, had killed Reilly.

Until now she had not seen that she had dragged the machine-gun butt with her when she jumped aside. The thing had swiveled neatly, and its bulky snout was centered on Abd el-Ulad's chest.

With strength which made her hands bend like willow twigs, she bore down on the trips.

The revolver exploded. With a small gasp and suddenly dulled eyes, she stared through the welter of flames which spat out before her.

Abd el-Ulad crumpled. His cloak was torn to ribbons. His chest was hammered into a mashed pulp. And the machine gun kept on firing, jolting the already dead body.

The belt ran out and the gun was silent. Kay stood swaying for a moment and then sagged, slowly, terribly, over the barrel of the weapon. The muzzle pointed toward the stars, small wisps of smoke curling out in lazy columns. A small red stream was turning the walnut grips a bright red.

A train was stopping at the station, brakes squealing, steam blowing and hissing. Men tumbled out to stand staring at the wreck that lay on the track, facing them. Turning, they saw the strewn bodies about the platform.

A Legion officer whistled. "By the good God, *mon général,* something has happened here!"

The general nodded. His head was shaped like a wedge and his lips were thin beneath chill eyes. Legionnaires eddied about him, staring at the wreckage.

General d'Avril, lately promoted to command of eastern Morocco, frowned. "There is something behind this, something I can't quite—" He looked into the shadow of the station. "There's one of them. Looks as if he's an officer, by the djellaba. See if he's alive."

They brought the man back and stretched him out. A surgeon knelt to listen to the heartbeats, and then nodded. "Yes, he's barely alive. Broken bones and a nasty cut in the side."

"Good lord!" cried d'Avril. "It's Reilly! Hell, man—he isn't going to die, he's too tough to kill! Get some bandages and some morphine and some— Get going! *Sacré nom d'un sacré chat bleu!* Look! Scatter about! That girl will be somewhere near at hand."

They scattered, and presently they came back, carrying her. D'Avril spread his cloak on the platform and they laid her gently upon it.

"She's got a bullet in the chest," announced the surgeon. "I can save her, perhaps, if I can get to a hospital in the next two hours."

"Well!" cried d'Avril. "What are we waiting for? I see what's happened here. We've got to get this man's story. He can save us hundreds of men and— Engineer! Start for Fez immediately."

Three weeks later, in an immaculate hospital ward in Fez, a man was wheeled into a private room. Through swathed bandages, half his face was visible—and half his Irish grin.

Propped up in bed by pillows, Kay MacArthur smiled and said, "How's the captain this morning? I didn't think they'd ever bring you in here to see me."

"Oh, I'll be out of this in a few days," said Reilly. "You can't keep a Mick down. How are you getting along?"

"Fine enough."

The intern wheeled the chair closer to the bedside. Reilly reached out and took Kay's hand. He was about to say something else when the door opened and d'Avril entered, rubbing his hands.

"Well, well, well! I see you've gotten together at last!" he beamed. "Reilly, my old, I could not wait to tell you! Acting on your information, we have everything on the windup. It's through, my boy—all the way through. The Riffs are going back to their homes in droves. We've confiscated all those guns we gave them and we're finished with the *Jihad*!"

"That's fine, General," said Reilly.

"How soon," said d'Avril, "do you think you can walk, my little cat?"

"In a week. She'll be up too."

"I wanted to know, because there's a little thing like a Commander's ribbon in the Legion of Honor coming up. It's the best thing to do, to wipe out all the past. They'll never say a word then."

"Don't I get my reward?" asked Kay.

D'Avril looked blank. "But ladies don't—"

Reilly grinned widely. In spite of the intern's protest, he leaned out of the wheel chair and planted a solid kiss upon her lips.

"Oh!" breathed d'Avril, looking human for once in his life. "Oh!" And he backed gracefully from the room.

Story Preview

Story Preview

NOW that you've just ventured through one of the captivating tales in the Stories from the Golden Age collection by L. Ron Hubbard, turn the page and enjoy a preview of *Yukon Madness*. Join Canadian Mountie Tommy McKenna as he stalks the trail of a brutal madman and his pack of bloodthirsty wolves across the frozen wilderness of the Yukon. But in order to get to his prey, he must first contend with the exotic and deceptive young woman, Kaja—a feat which may just prove deadly.

Yukon Madness

I TAUK THE MADMAN, stalking across the bitter wastes, squinting with slanted eyes over the backs of his twelve-wolf team, stared into the blackness toward the snarling flares of red and green and white which shot into the indigo winter sky—the aurora borealis. Itauk the Madman, a horror in the raw north of Hudson Bay, spreading death with sharp steel and throwing the shattered bodies of men to his slavering team.

Twelve wolves as black as the winter sky, glittering teeth as sharp as the white ice which jutted through the dry snow, mouths as red-flecked as the borealis, tugged at the sledge traces. And Itauk laughed—a piercing, grating laughter which splintered the great silence.

Tommy McKenna heard the laugh, though it was far away. And Tommy McKenna shuddered under his red coat and sealskin parka. He could see nothing, but he heard. The cold barrel of the Lee-Enfield was hard under his tight fingers. His eyes—gray eyes as cold as arctic ice—closed to lines.

That was Itauk. The sound came far through the ebon chill. That was Itauk and Billy Simmons was back at camp alone, sleeping. Or was he sleeping still? Had Itauk struck again in the Yukon Territory?

Tommy McKenna raised his snowshoes and struck out

in a rapid lope for camp. He had forgotten the bear tracks he had seen earlier in the day. He had forgotten that he and Simmons were almost out of food. He remembered only his charge to "get his man."

"Get Itauk!" the lieutenant had ordered at Post Ledoux. It had sent McKenna and Simmons on a five-hundred-mile trek through blackness, through acid cold, across uncharted seas of snow.

And now Itauk's laugh out of the ebon cold. Tommy McKenna's snowshoes rapped the dry crust in a steady tempo. His lean, weathered face—handsome before it had been too long exposed to screaming winds and silent mountains of white—was almost buried in the fur hood. It was fifty-five below and a man's breath froze in his nostrils and stayed there, freezing his lungs.

He came within a hundred yards of the camp and stopped. He called out, his voice clear as a trumpet, "Simmons!"

No answer. Heavy, throbbing silence. The flare and flash of the northern lights as they shot spitefully up at the stars. A wolf howled out in the cold alone, dismal and quavering. Answering the call.

Calling "Simmons!" again, he listened intently.

Tommy McKenna threw off the safety of the Enfield. His mittens were clumsy but he dared not take them off. His hands would freeze to the barrel of his gun.

"Simmons!"

Uncertain now. Knowledge as icy as the half-year night told Tommy McKenna that he would never again hear Simmons' voice. With that sixth or perhaps seventh sense born in men who stand eye to eye with danger and the raw North, Tommy McKenna already understood.

He advanced slowly. The fire was a red glow against the blue darkness. The flame had died down. A shadow lay against it, a shadow queerly limp and empty.

Tommy McKenna stared at the patch of scarlet cloth. A bright warm stain was growing in the dry snow, spreading out slowly and steadily.

Simmons' face had been torn away as though by claws. Nothing remained but the broken, red-shredded skull. Tufts of his parka lay black against the white. Blood was scattered far.

Tommy McKenna's voice was stiff, unreal. "He . . . turned his wolves . . . to feast . . ."

Anger blocked out the body, blacked the northern lights. Tommy's hands shook with rage. He looked north and his eyes were chill.

The unwritten law of the Mounties: Swift death to those who would kill one of us.

Itauk would die. With either bullets or steel or bare hands. No trial for Itauk now. He had committed the unforgivable crime, punishable by instant death on sight. He had killed Simmons of the Royal Canadian Mounted Police. No wooden gallows in the Yukon Territory headquarters, with a priest to see Itauk through death's door; it had to come when—and as soon as death could!

Tommy McKenna looked back at the fire. The torn fur and scattered bones of the sledge dogs told a swift story. Tommy knew that he was on foot, that he would have to live from kill to kill—unless he met Itauk.

The garish flame of the northern lights showed up the trail. The large pads of Itauk's wolves had left their plain print upon the snow, and over the pads was the print of a *kamik*-covered foot. That was Itauk.

Picking up a bundle of supplies from the ruin of their outfit, Tommy struck out. His snowshoes rasped over the dry cold surface and the weight of the Enfield was hard against his arm. No time to bury Simmons now. The pause might lose him his quarry.

Slogging through the never-ending night, Tommy heard the sounds of the North: the crackle of ice under terrific stress; the moan of sharp wind across the great reaches; the shivering hunting cry of the wolf.

For hours the trail was straight, leading into the very heart of the borealis. Itauk the Madman was traveling fast and far, lengthening the road which was milestoned with blood.

Tommy's breath was ice on his lips and his lungs burned from exertion and freezing air. The Enfield grew heavier. The revolver under the parka banged with steady monotony against his thigh.

His squinted eyes did not leave the trail. The sound of his snowshoes was like the staccato flicking of sandpaper across a drumhead.

He stopped, still looking down, his practiced glance reading the story.

Someone had intercepted Itauk's trail. The sledge had stopped. Then a pair of shoes led off at an angle, traveling west.

To find out more about *Yukon Madness* and how you can obtain your copy, go to www.goldenagestories.com.

Glossary

Glossary

STORIES FROM THE GOLDEN AGE *reflect the words and expressions used in the 1930s and 1940s, adding unique flavor and authenticity to the tales. While a character's speech may often reflect regional origins, it also can convey attitudes common in the day. So that readers can better grasp such cultural and historical terms, uncommon words or expressions of the era, the following glossary has been provided.*

Abd el-Krim: (1882–1963) the Berber leader of the Rif, a Berber area of northeastern Morocco. He became the leader of a wide-scale armed resistance movement against French and Spanish colonial rule in North Africa. His guerilla tactics are known to have inspired others.

Atlas: Atlas Mountains; a mountain range in northwest Africa extending about fifteen hundred miles through Morocco, Algeria and Tunisia, including the Rock of Gibraltar. The Atlas range separates the Mediterranean and Atlantic coastlines from the Sahara Desert.

barbs: a breed of horses introduced by the Moors (Muslim people of mixed Berber and Arab descent) that resemble Arabian horses and are known for their speed and endurance.

bataillon pénal: (French) penal battalion; military unit consisting of convicted persons for whom military service was either assigned punishment or a voluntary replacement of imprisonment. Penal battalion service was very dangerous: the official view was that they were highly expendable and were to be used to reduce losses in regular units. Convicts were released from their term of service early if they suffered a combat injury (the crime was considered to be "washed out with blood") or performed a heroic deed.

Berber: a member of a people living in North Africa, primarily Muslim, living in settled or nomadic tribes between the Sahara and Mediterranean Sea and between Egypt and the Atlantic Ocean.

bled: a prairie or treeless plain in northern Africa; countryside.

cacolets: (French) horse or mule litters for the transport of wounded.

call to colors: the ceremony of hoisting the national flag at 8:00 AM and of lowering it at sunset, the sounding of a bugle being part of each ceremony.

cantle: the raised back part of a saddle for a horse.

Casablanca: a seaport on the Atlantic coast of Morocco.

Chasseurs Alpins: (French) Alpine Hunters or Alpine Chasers; the mountain infantry and an elite unit of the French Army. They are trained to operate in mountainous terrain and in urban warfare.

djellaba: a long loose hooded garment with full sleeves, worn especially in Muslim countries.

en avant: (French) forward.

Fez: the former capital of several dynasties and one of the holiest places in Morocco; it has kept its religious primacy through the ages.

flintlock: a type of gun fired by a spark from a flint (rock used with steel to produce an igniting spark). It was introduced about 1630.

Franzawi: (Arabic) Frenchman.

G-men: government men; agents of the Federal Bureau of Investigation.

hard-boiled: tough; unsentimental.

High Atlas: portion of the Atlas Mountain range that rises in the west at the Atlantic coast and stretches in an eastern direction to the Moroccan-Algerian border.

hobnail: a short nail with a thick head used to increase the durability of a boot sole.

horns of Ramadan: the horns blown each morning during Ramadan, a sacred month in the Islamic faith.

Hudson Bay: a large inland sea in the northeast of Canada. On the east it is connected with the Atlantic Ocean and on the north with the Arctic Ocean.

Irish Guard: a military unit in the French Army composed of Irish exiles. It was formed in 1690 and for one hundred years served the French Army. In battle they won glory and highest honors for themselves and Ireland and the undying respect of friend and foe. When the Irish Guard was dissolved they were presented with a special flag from the French government bearing the Irish Harp embroidered with shamrocks and fleurs-de-lis and touted with honors for their service to France.

kamik: (Eskimo) a knee-high waterproof boot with a hard sole, made of sealskin.

la belle Légion: (French) the lovely Legion.

Lebel: a French rifle that was adopted as a standard infantry weapon in 1887 and remained in official service until after World War II.

Lee-Enfield: a standard bolt-action magazine-fed repeating rifle; the British Army's standard rifle for over sixty years from 1895 until 1956, although it remained in British service well into the early 1960s and is still found in service in the armed forces of some Commonwealth nations.

Legionnaire: a member of the French Foreign Legion, a unique elite unit within the French Army established in 1831. It was created as a unit for foreign volunteers and was primarily used to protect and expand the French colonial empire during the nineteenth century, but has also taken part in all of France's wars with other European powers. It is known to be an elite military unit whose training focuses not only on traditional military skills, but also on the building of a strong *esprit de corps* amongst members. As its men come from different countries with different cultures, this is a widely accepted solution to strengthen them enough to work as a team. Training is often not only physically hard with brutal training methods, but also extremely stressful with high rates of desertion.

Mannlicher: a type of rifle equipped with a manually operated sliding bolt for loading cartridges for firing, as opposed to the more common rotating bolt of other rifles. Mannlicher rifles were considered reasonably strong and accurate.

Mauser: a bolt-action rifle made by Mauser, a German arms manufacturer. These rifles have been made since the 1870s.

Meknes: a city in northern Morocco.

Melilla: a Spanish enclave (a country or part of a country mostly surrounded by or wholly lying within the boundaries of another country) on the Mediterranean Rif coast of North Africa, neighboring Morocco.

Mick: term for a person of Irish birth or descent.

mon Dieu: (French) my God.

Morocco: a country of northwest Africa on the Mediterranean Sea and the Atlantic Ocean. The French established a protectorate over most of the region in 1912, and in 1956 Morocco achieved independence as a kingdom.

musette: a small canvas or leather bag with a shoulder strap, as one used by soldiers or travelers.

old, my: used as a term of cordiality and familiarity.

PC: Post Command; military installation where the command personnel are located.

Riff or **Riffian:** a member of any of several Berber peoples inhabiting the Er Rif, a hilly region along the coast of northern Morocco. The Berber people of the area remained fiercely independent until they were subdued by French and Spanish forces (1925–1926).

route step: a normal pace in marching in which it is not necessary to march in step. Used mainly in the field when moving from place to place as a unit.

sacrebleu: (French) used as a mild oath to express surprise or annoyance.

Sacré nom d'un sacré chat bleu!: (French) Sacred name of a sacred blue cat!

Scheherazade: the female narrator of *The Arabian Nights,* who during one thousand and one adventurous nights saved her life by entertaining her husband, the king, with stories.

Senegalese: people of Senegal, on the western coast of Africa. Senegal was awarded to France in 1815 by the Treaty of Paris and became a French colony in 1895 as part of French West Africa, with full independence being won in 1960.

Shilha: the Berber dialect spoken in the mountains of southern Morocco.

sīdī: (Arabic) 1. an African Muslim holding a high position under a king. 2. used as a title of respect; sir; master.

Sidi-bel-Abbès: the capital of the Sidi-bel-Abbès province in northwestern Algeria. The city was developed around a French camp built in 1843. From 1931 until 1961, the city was the "holy city" or spiritual home of the French Foreign Legion, the location of its basic training camp and the headquarters of its first foreign regiment.

Snider: a rifle formerly used in the British service. It was invented by American Jacob Snider in the mid-1800s. The Snider was a breech-loading rifle, derived from its muzzle-loading predecessor called the Enfield.

Spahis: light cavalry regiments of the French Army recruited primarily from Algeria, Tunisia and Morocco.

St. Cyr: a community in the western suburbs of Paris, France. It used to host the training school for officers of the French Army.

tricolor: the French national flag, consisting of three equal vertical bands of blue, white and red.

Tuaregs: members of the nomadic Berber-speaking people of the southwestern Sahara in Africa. They have traditionally engaged in herding, agriculture and convoying caravans across their territories. The Tuaregs became among the most hostile of all the colonized peoples of French West Africa, because they were among the most affected by colonial policies. In 1917, they fought a vicious and bloody war against the French, but they were defeated and as a result, dispossessed of traditional grazing lands. They are known to be fierce warriors; European explorers expressed their fear by warning, "The scorpion and the Tuareg are the only enemies you meet in the desert."

Vega: the fifth brightest of all stars and the third brightest in the northern sky.

Yukon Territory: the westernmost of Canada's three territories, it is positioned in the northwest corner, bordering Alaska. Yukon is known as "the land of the midnight sun" because for three months in summer, sunlight is almost continuous. In winter, however, darkness sets in and the light of day is not seen for a quarter of the year.

Zephyrs: penal battalions for the French Foreign Legion; nickname given in Algeria to a corps that is recruited from the French Army, those who would not conform to discipline or who were criminals. This punishment, no matter its length, does not count in the term of military duty which the state requires.

zut: (French) damn.

L. Ron Hubbard
in the Golden Age
of Pulp Fiction

*In writing an adventure story
a writer has to know that he is adventuring
for a lot of people who cannot.
The writer has to take them here and there
about the globe and show them
excitement and love and realism.
As long as that writer is living the part of an
adventurer when he is hammering
the keys, he is succeeding with his story.*

*Adventuring is a state of mind.
If you adventure through life, you have a
good chance to be a success on paper.*

*Adventure doesn't mean globe-trotting,
exactly, and it doesn't mean great deeds.
Adventuring is like art.
You have to live it to make it real.*

—L. RON HUBBARD

L. Ron Hubbard
and American
Pulp Fiction

ORN March 13, 1911, L. Ron Hubbard lived a life at
least as expansive as the stories with which he enthralled
a hundred million readers through a fifty-year career.

Originally hailing from Tilden, Nebraska, he spent his
formative years in a classically rugged Montana, replete with
the cowpunchers, lawmen and desperadoes who would later
people his Wild West adventures. And lest anyone imagine
those adventures were drawn from vicarious experience, he
was not only breaking broncs at a tender age, he was also
among the few whites ever admitted into Blackfoot society
as a bona fide blood brother. While if only to round out an
otherwise rough and tumble youth, his mother was that rarity
of her time—a thoroughly educated woman—who introduced
her son to the classics of Occidental literature even before
his seventh birthday.

But as any dedicated L. Ron Hubbard reader will attest, his
world extended far beyond Montana. In point of fact, and as the
son of a United States naval officer, by the age of eighteen he
had traveled over a quarter of a million miles. Included therein
were three Pacific crossings to a then still mysterious Asia, where
he ran with the likes of Her British Majesty's agent-in-place

for North China, and the last in the line of Royal Magicians from the court of Kublai Khan. For the record, L. Ron Hubbard was also among the first Westerners to gain admittance to forbidden Tibetan monasteries below Manchuria, and his photographs of China's Great Wall long graced American geography texts.

L. Ron Hubbard, left, at Congressional Airport, Washington, DC, 1931, with members of George Washington University flying club.

Upon his return to the United States and a hasty completion of his interrupted high school education, the young Ron Hubbard entered George Washington University. There, as fans of his aerial adventures may have heard, he earned his wings as a pioneering barnstormer at the dawn of American aviation. He also earned a place in free-flight record books for the longest sustained flight above Chicago. Moreover, as a roving reporter for *Sportsman Pilot* (featuring his first professionally penned articles), he further helped inspire a generation of pilots who would take America to world airpower.

Immediately beyond his sophomore year, Ron embarked on the first of his famed ethnological expeditions, initially to then untrammeled Caribbean shores (descriptions of which would later fill a whole series of West Indies mystery-thrillers). That the Puerto Rican interior would also figure into the future of Ron Hubbard stories was likewise no accident. For in addition to cultural studies of the island, a 1932–33

LRH expedition is rightly remembered as conducting the first complete mineralogical survey of a Puerto Rico under United States jurisdiction.

There was many another adventure along this vein: As a lifetime member of the famed Explorers Club, L. Ron Hubbard charted North Pacific waters with the first shipboard radio direction finder, and so pioneered a long-range navigation system universally employed until the late twentieth century. While not to put too fine an edge on it, he also held a rare Master Mariner's license to pilot any vessel, of any tonnage in any ocean.

Yet lest we stray too far afield, there is an LRH note at this juncture in his saga, and it reads in part:

"I started out writing for the pulps, writing the best I knew, writing for every mag on the stands, slanting as well as I could."

To which one might add: His earliest submissions date from the

Capt. L. Ron Hubbard in Ketchikan, Alaska, 1940, on his Alaskan Radio Experimental Expedition, the first of three voyages conducted under the Explorers Club flag.

summer of 1934, and included tales drawn from true-to-life Asian adventures, with characters roughly modeled on British/American intelligence operatives he had known in Shanghai. His early Westerns were similarly peppered with details drawn from personal experience. Although therein lay a first hard lesson from the often cruel world of the pulps. His first Westerns were soundly rejected as lacking the authenticity of a Max Brand yarn (a particularly frustrating comment given L. Ron Hubbard's Westerns came straight from his Montana homeland, while Max Brand was a mediocre New York poet named Frederick Schiller Faust, who turned out implausible six-shooter tales from the terrace of an Italian villa).

Nevertheless, and needless to say, L. Ron Hubbard persevered and soon earned a reputation as among the most publishable names in pulp fiction, with a ninety percent placement rate of first-draft manuscripts. He was also among the most prolific, averaging between seventy and a hundred thousand words a month. Hence the rumors that L. Ron Hubbard had redesigned a typewriter for faster keyboard action and pounded out manuscripts on a continuous roll of butcher paper to save the precious seconds it took to insert a single sheet of paper into manual typewriters of the day.

That all L. Ron Hubbard stories did not run beneath said byline is yet another aspect of pulp fiction lore. That is, as publishers periodically rejected manuscripts from top-drawer authors if only to avoid paying top dollar, L. Ron Hubbard and company just as frequently replied with submissions under various pseudonyms. In Ron's case, the

A MAN OF MANY NAMES

Between 1934 and 1950, L. Ron Hubbard authored more than fifteen million words of fiction in more than two hundred classic publications. To supply his fans and editors with stories across an array of genres and pulp titles, he adopted fifteen pseudonyms in addition to his already renowned L. Ron Hubbard byline.

Winchester Remington Colt
Lt. Jonathan Daly
Capt. Charles Gordon
Capt. L. Ron Hubbard
Bernard Hubbel
Michael Keith
Rene Lafayette
Legionnaire 148
Legionnaire 14830
Ken Martin
Scott Morgan
Lt. Scott Morgan
Kurt von Rachen
Barry Randolph
Capt. Humbert Reynolds

list included: Rene Lafayette, Captain Charles Gordon, Lt. Scott Morgan and the notorious Kurt von Rachen—supposedly on the lam for a murder rap, while hammering out two-fisted prose in Argentina. The point: While L. Ron Hubbard as Ken Martin spun stories of Southeast Asian intrigue, LRH as Barry Randolph authored tales of

L. Ron Hubbard, circa 1930, at the outset of a literary career that would finally span half a century.

romance on the Western range—which, stretching between a dozen genres is how he came to stand among the two hundred elite authors providing close to a million tales through the glory days of American Pulp Fiction.

In evidence of exactly that, by 1936 L. Ron Hubbard was literally leading pulp fiction's elite as president of New York's American Fiction Guild. Members included a veritable pulp hall of fame: Lester "Doc Savage" Dent, Walter "The Shadow" Gibson, and the legendary Dashiell Hammett—to cite but a few.

Also in evidence of just where L. Ron Hubbard stood within his first two years on the American pulp circuit: By the spring of 1937, he was ensconced in Hollywood, adopting a Caribbean thriller for Columbia Pictures, remembered today as *The Secret of Treasure Island*. Comprising fifteen thirty-minute episodes, the L. Ron Hubbard screenplay led to the most profitable matinée serial in Hollywood history. In accord with Hollywood culture, he was thereafter continually called upon

The 1937 Secret of Treasure Island, *a fifteen-episode serial adapted for the screen by L. Ron Hubbard from his novel,* Murder at Pirate Castle.

to rewrite/doctor scripts—most famously for long-time friend and fellow adventurer Clark Gable.

In the interim—and herein lies another distinctive chapter of the L. Ron Hubbard story—he continually worked to open Pulp Kingdom gates to up-and-coming authors. Or, for that matter, anyone who wished to write. It was a fairly unconventional stance, as markets were already thin and competition razor sharp. But the fact remains, it was an L. Ron Hubbard hallmark that he vehemently lobbied on behalf of young authors—regularly supplying instructional articles to trade journals, guest-lecturing to short story classes at George Washington University and Harvard, and even founding his own creative writing competition. It was established in 1940, dubbed the Golden Pen, and guaranteed winners both New York representation and publication in *Argosy*.

But it was John W. Campbell Jr.'s *Astounding Science Fiction* that finally proved the most memorable LRH vehicle. While every fan of L. Ron Hubbard's galactic epics undoubtedly knows the story, it nonetheless bears repeating: By late 1938, the pulp publishing magnate of Street & Smith was determined to revamp *Astounding Science Fiction* for broader readership. In particular, senior editorial director F. Orlin Tremaine called for stories with a stronger *human element*. When acting editor John W. Campbell balked, preferring his spaceship-driven tales, Tremaine enlisted Hubbard. Hubbard, in turn, replied with the genre's first truly *character-driven* works, wherein heroes are pitted not against bug-eyed monsters but the mystery and majesty of deep space itself—and thus was launched the Golden Age of Science Fiction.

The names alone are enough to quicken the pulse of any science fiction aficionado, including LRH friend and protégé, Robert Heinlein, Isaac Asimov, A. E. van Vogt and Ray Bradbury. Moreover, when coupled with LRH stories of fantasy, we further come to what's rightly been described as the foundation of every modern tale of horror: L. Ron Hubbard's immortal *Fear.* It was rightly proclaimed by Stephen King as one of the very few works to genuinely warrant that overworked term "classic"—as in: *"This is a classic tale of creeping, surreal menace and horror. . . . This is one of the really, really good ones."*

To accommodate the greater body of L. Ron Hubbard fantasies, Street & Smith inaugurated *Unknown*—a classic pulp if there ever was one, and wherein readers were soon thrilling to the likes of *Typewriter in the Sky* and *Slaves of Sleep* of which Frederik Pohl would declare: *"There are bits and pieces from Ron's work that became part of the language in ways that very few other writers managed."*

And, indeed, at J. W. Campbell Jr.'s insistence, Ron was regularly drawing on themes from the Arabian Nights and

L. Ron Hubbard, 1948, among fellow science fiction luminaries at the World Science Fiction Convention in Toronto.

so introducing readers to a world of genies, jinn, Aladdin and Sinbad—all of which, of course, continue to float through cultural mythology to this day.

At least as influential in terms of post-apocalypse stories was L. Ron Hubbard's 1940 *Final Blackout*. Generally acclaimed as the finest anti-war novel of the decade and among the ten best works of the genre ever authored—here, too, was a tale that would live on in ways few other writers imagined.

Hence, the later Robert Heinlein verdict: "Final Blackout *is as perfect a piece of science fiction as has ever been written.*"

Like many another who both lived and wrote American pulp adventure, the war proved a tragic end to Ron's sojourn in the pulps. He served with distinction in four theaters and was highly decorated for commanding corvettes in the North Pacific. He was also grievously wounded in combat, lost many a close friend and colleague and thus resolved to say farewell to pulp fiction and devote himself to what it had supported these many years—namely, his serious research.

Portland, Oregon, 1943; L. Ron Hubbard, captain of the US Navy subchaser PC 815.

But in no way was the LRH literary saga at an end, for as he wrote some thirty years later, in 1980:

"Recently there came a period when I had little to do. This was novel in a life so crammed with busy years, and I decided to amuse myself by writing a novel that was pure *science fiction."*

That work was *Battlefield Earth: A Saga of the Year 3000*. It was an immediate *New York Times* bestseller and, in fact, the first international science fiction blockbuster in decades. It was not, however, L. Ron Hubbard's magnum opus, as that distinction is generally reserved for his next and final work: The 1.2 million word *Mission Earth*.

> **Final Blackout** *is as perfect a piece of science fiction as has ever been written.*
>
> —**Robert Heinlein**

How he managed those 1.2 million words in just over twelve months is yet another piece of the L. Ron Hubbard legend. But the fact remains, he did indeed author a ten-volume *dekalogy* that lives in publishing history for the fact that each and every volume of the series was also a *New York Times* bestseller.

Moreover, as subsequent generations discovered L. Ron Hubbard through republished works and novelizations of his screenplays, the mere fact of his name on a cover signaled an international bestseller. . . . Until, to date, sales of his works exceed hundreds of millions, and he otherwise remains among the most enduring and widely read authors in literary history. Although as a final word on the tales of L. Ron Hubbard, perhaps it's enough to simply reiterate what editors told readers in the glory days of American Pulp Fiction:

He writes the way he does, brothers, because he's been there, seen it and done it!

THE STORIES FROM THE GOLDEN AGE

Your ticket to adventure starts here with the Stories from
the Golden Age collection by master storyteller L. Ron Hubbard.
These gripping tales are set in a kaleidoscope of exotic locales and brim
with fascinating characters, including some of the
most vile villains, dangerous dames and brazen heroes
you'll ever get to meet.

The entire collection of over one hundred and fifty stories is being
released in a series of eighty books and audiobooks.
For an up-to-date listing of available titles,
go to www.goldenagestories.com.

AIR ADVENTURE

FAR-FLUNG ADVENTURE

SEA ADVENTURE

TALES FROM THE ORIENT

The Devil—With Wings   *Pearl Pirate*
The Falcon Killer   *The Red Dragon*
Five Mex for a Million   *Spy Killer*
Golden Hell   *Tah*
The Green God   *The Trail of the Red Diamonds*
Hurricane's Roar   *Wind-Gone-Mad*
Inky Odds   *Yellow Loot*
Orders Is Orders

MYSTERY

The Blow Torch Murder   *The Grease Spot*
Brass Keys to Murder   *Killer Ape*
Calling Squad Cars!   *Killer's Law*
The Carnival of Death   *The Mad Dog Murder*
The Chee-Chalker   *Mouthpiece*
Dead Men Kill   *Murder Afloat*
The Death Flyer   *The Slickers*
Flame City   *They Killed Him Dead*

FANTASY

Borrowed Glory   *If I Were You*
The Crossroads   *The Last Drop*
Danger in the Dark   *The Room*
The Devil's Rescue   *The Tramp*
He Didn't Like Cats

SCIENCE FICTION

The Automagic Horse   *A Matter of Matter*
Battle of Wizards   *The Obsolete Weapon*
Battling Bolto   *One Was Stubborn*
The Beast   *The Planet Makers*
Beyond All Weapons   *The Professor Was a Thief*
A Can of Vacuum   *The Slaver*
The Conroy Diary   *Space Can*
The Dangerous Dimension   *Strain*
Final Enemy   *Tough Old Man*
The Great Secret   *240,000 Miles Straight Up*
Greed   *When Shadows Fall*
The Invaders

120

WESTERN

JOIN THE PULP REVIVAL
America in the 1930s and 40s

Pulp fiction was in its heyday and 30 million readers were regularly riveted by the larger-than-life tales of master storyteller L. Ron Hubbard. For this was pulp fiction's golden age, when the writing was raw and every page packed a walloping punch.

That magic can now be yours. An evocative world of nefarious villains, exotic intrigues, courageous heroes and heroines—a world that today's cinema has barely tapped for tales of adventure and swashbucklers.

Enroll today in the Stories from the Golden Age Club and begin receiving your monthly feature edition selected from more than 150 stories in the collection.

You may choose to enjoy them as either a paperback or audiobook for the special membership price of $9.95 each month along with FREE shipping and handling.